Life on the Run

JOE FRAZIER

WWW.JOEFRAZIERPRODUCTIONS.COM

PUBLISHER'S NOTE:

This book is a work of fiction. Names, Characters, places and incidents are products of the imagination. Or used fictitiously any resemblance to actual events or locals or persons living or dead, is entirely coincidental.

ISBN-13: 978-0-692-75165-7

Library of Congress Catalog Card Number: In publication data.

Life on the Run

Written by: Joe Frazier

Edited by: It's The Write Stuff & Joe Frazier

Text Formation: Complete Steps Publishing, LLC

Cover Design and Layout: Dynasty's Cover Me

Printed in the United States of America

Dedication

I dedicate this book to the youth that's easily distracted
away from the most valuable keys of their lives which would
first be an education, when you derail from the right way to
live you drift into the dark, where there's lies, false hope
and contaminated success, and majority of time you don't
even realize that your life has took a turn for the worst, the
number one curse will always be the enemy, is inherited
negatively, I also dedicate this book to those who lost their
lives and never had a chance to have a new beginning, in
this day in time you definitely have to analyze what's in
your hand before you sign because one thing about this life
we living, is that it comes with novels of fine print
something we don't really have the patience to read,
regardless of what you have or don't have maintain your
patience with the right way to
live and you will have more than what you thought you
deserve...

Author Joe Frazier

Acknowledgements

I would like to send a special thank you to the streets of North Philly, for molding me mentally into wanting something better out of life. I would like to thank my teachers at William D. Kelly Elementary for putting words of wisdom in my head that I still remember to this day. Thank you to my mother and everyone that believe in me while the doubters doubted me, you continue to see my vision and for that I am thankful. A special shout out to my kids Jamal; Wilson, Alexsus Frazier, and Nevaeh Frazier for making me feel like I needed more than a 9-5 to make you all happy. Last but not least, my fans that enjoy my personality and sense of humor. I thank you for supporting me on this publishing journey.

CHAPTER 1

It's September 7, 2010, the first day of school. My alarm is ringing and I'm ready to throw this muthafucka, because I don't know how to cut it off. I don't have any new school clothes; I'm too ashamed to go, and just when I thought the morning couldn't get any worse, here comes Mom with her shit.

"Amin, come on get up. It's time to go learn some shit. Don't just lay there either like you don't hear me or that alarm, you forgot who I am nigga?"

I finally found the snooze button and fell back for another five minutes, but awe shit here she comes.

Before I can get the covers off, my mom threw a bucket of cold ass water on me.

"Damn Mom, what the fuck?"

"Whoa, nigga, did you just cuss at me, or am I hearing shit?" Amin I think I heard some shit." When I get up out the bed my mom hit me with an educated six – piece, two jabs, a hook, with three uppercuts sending me into a balled-up shell, if i knew she felt like that this morning i would've been up before my alarm went off.

Pearl always had a fast temper, if she's in the middle of an argument; she always threw the first blow. However, if she didn't feel like fighting, she would grab you, and then stab you.

"Now nigga! You got another bucket waiting on that ass tomorrow! Who the fuck you think you talking to?"

I can feel my face swelling up as I gently touch it, at the same time I'm looking at the shit I had on yesterday, laid out on the ironing board, with the same water ice and pretzel stains still there. Shaking my head, I wonder if she's serious, because I'll be damned if I'm showing up for school looking broke, with a beat-up face, and yesterday's clothes on, all at the same time, shit that's a bit too much.

Leaving the house, I'm embarrassed as hell, because people saw this Polo outfit yesterday when I thought I was cute. Now I'm on my way to school with yesterday's dirty clothes on, and on top of that, a new accessory. A colorful black eye, my mom is the best that ever did it I tell you.

Sometimes I even wonder if she's the fuck crazy.

We live in North Philly, on a nice quiet block, 30th Street off of Jefferson, but when you turn the corner, it's a totally different scene. As I turn the corner walking with my head down, a familiar voice calls my name out. When I raise my head, it's my main man. Damien. Damien is my classmate from last year, a good dude that was real with it from day one.

"Yo, what's up, Amin?"

"Ain't too much, what you up to?"

"Ain't shit, just burning time for my girl's mom to go to work, so I can get in some pussy and be all in love for a minute. Oh shit, yo, who were you fighting?"

"Yo, my mom teed off on me this morning, because I didn't get out the bed when my alarm went off. She had a nerve to be bobbing' and weaving wit' the shit, man. My mom funny as shit, yo!"

"Yo, ya mom nice with it, but why the fuck you ain't duck, nigga?" you was supposed to duck if you seen all that shit coming."

"That shit came too fast, Damien. I wasn't expecting to

get beat the fuck up soon as I woke up, nigga."

"Aye, Amin, hold up this shit ain't unbelievable, this shit is unbeweaveable.

"My nigga, how you get beat up in your sleep, when you wasn't even woke yet, nigga?" Damien breaks out and starts laughing so hard, to the point where I found the shit funny because i can hear it in his voice that he couldn't help it.

"Yo, you really going to school looking like Martin, Amin?"

"I wish I didn't have to."

"Well shit come to think about it, Amin, Diamond just moved her girlfriend in and she is drop dead gorgeous. She's kinda stressed too, so all you gotta do is be real with her and become somebody she can talk to. She'll probably fuck you, and if she do, yo, fuck her like it's the last piece of pussy on earth. Lock that pussy down so you can have somebody to talk to, because I'm not trying to hear that shit. Sike homie, I'm just bullshitting; it's whatever, you already."

Just the thought of being in the presence of beautiful women gives me the chills. These stains in my pants are spelling me out to be on some ol' dirty shit, but fuck it. I'm still well respected, due to my big cousin, Moncho, not playing any games out here. He's not-flashy, but he's working with a hundred thousand dollars at only nineteen.

CHAPTER 2

"Come on, Amin, let's get off Jefferson Street before big Pearl turns this corner and fucks you up again!"

"I ain't tryna hear that shit, Damien, my face hurt." Yeah, your mom's outta order for that, 'specially 'cause it's the first day of school. Yo, not to be in your biz, but do she get high?"

"Naw, why you ask?" "You don't know, your mom has a violent reputation? Your mom stabbed the cashier in the supermarket back in the day for getting smart, so whatever you did, I wouldn't do that shit no more."

Damn, I almost forgot our moms attended Strawberry Mansion School together. I guess he knows all about that three to six years she did, even though she told me she was fighting a war overseas.

"Yeah, I knew about that, Damien. I was about eight when the cops kicked our door down took her away, and told me she'd be back later."

"Yo, I can tell that just touched you too. I see your eyes watering, you bitch ass nigga."

"Fuck you, Damien. Let Margaret get booked, bitch; that'll touch you too. Come to think of it, ya mom gotta old ass name; she sound like one of them old ladies that used to give out the free lunches in the late 1860's."

"No, you didn't just say that."

"Yeah I did Damien, and the last muthafucka that said, 'Oh no you just didn't say that', hit me with some shit, so I'm ready for that ass. Bus' a move, muthafucka."

"Naw, we don't have to go there, Amin, we about to take it right here."

When I realized that we were at Diamond's house, my heart just dropped, I'm wondering if they gonna look at me as the dirty dude.

Diamond came to the window looking like a Puerto Rican Halle Berry fresh out the shower, giving me the "who the fuck is you" look.

"Hey baby, I'll be right down."

"Yo, you see that, Amin?"

"Fo' sho' my nigga. She's tough, but don't be all wanting to jump off a bridge about this bitch nigga you know it's always good in the beginning."

"Amin i get pussy, i don't get emotional nigga, now before i was rudely interrupted her girlfriend Karen looks better. Just keep your style original, they hate them wannabe ass niggas, Amin."

"Shit, me too."

"Yeah, here she comes now, yo."

Diamond opens the door in a white Polo robe with the shower shoes to match. She offers me a warm welcoming displaying a real smile, as she holds the door for me to come in.

"Hello, and your name is?"

"I'm Amin."

She gives me her hand to shake. "Pleased to meet you, I'm Damo's girlfriend, Diamond."

"Likewise."

"Fuck you mean likewise? You his girlfriend too?"

"Sike, I'm just playin'."
"Damien, can you please tell me when you're bringing company? No offense,

Amin."

"I'm good love."

"Well, come on in and relax. I got my sister, Karen, to keep you company. Would you like anything to drink or snack on?"

"Hell Yeah, I'll take a sausage, egg, and cheese, a medium orange juice, and a Newport one hundred, shit treat a nigga right."

"Aye Damien where you find this nigga, is he serious?" no Damien I'm not laughing."

"No, my man just silly. But yo we're you serious?" "You think I'm bullshittin'? Sike, no thank you, but thank you anyway,

Diamond."

"You're welcome and Amin, you can call me Dee."

"Okay, Dee it is."

I hear someone coming down the steps, and my heart started thumping. This must be Karen. I turn around and locked eyes with a very attractive woman and couldn't shy away because the beauty in her eyes had me paralyzed from the neck up, but i also can tell she seen something she like at the same time.

"Hey you two, y'all could've told me it was company down here."

"Aw, that's some bullshit. You must like him already, because I told you upstairs that we were having company."

"Diamond, cut it out."

"Hello, my name is Karen and yours?"

"Amin, and pleased to meet you, Karen."

"Same here. Well Diamond, is you staying downstairs?"

"No, I need some water before I come up. Y'all can go get to know each other a lil' bit. We'll be up in a little while."

"Okay, come on up, Amin."

I'm at my greatest trying to act like this is what the fuck i do but it's too late to turn back.

Karen has black, silky shoulder-length hair and appears to be a blend of Indian and African American, but more Indian, with a warm delicious caramel complexion, her beauty is intimidating. This girl looks amazing! Man, fuck this stain; I'm about to dish out my A-game!

When I see Karen has her own room, I started strolling a lil' bit, like I just know I'm about to get some pussy. Karen comes in and shut the door, as I'm wondering how this is about to go down.

"So Amin, what's so boring about the first day of school?"

"Baby I think my mom fucked that check up because she didn't grab me no school clothes, and then she spazzed on me on some early in the morning shit. Check me out."

"Damn, I guess you as real as they come, because I believe you. Wow, yo, that was a lot to share with me on the first one-on-one."

"Yeah, well, this shit bothers me."

"Well, just know that if it bothers you; you will fix that issue all by yourself. I don't look at you funny, because you kept it real and got beat up this morning. It just tells me I gotta money hungry nigga that need to at least move out the way when you see that shit coming next time. It looks like you just stood there and let her fuck you up, and sometimes that make the ass whipping last longer. No baby, I know a bum when I see one and you're not a bum; you just can't help the situation right now...okay handsome?"

I remain silent as I'm thinking about what she said. It makes sense because if I'm comfortable with not having the things I'm supposed to, who would I become then? If there are no positive adults around to check you on time, there's no telling what you'll be when you grow up.

Karen made me feel more comfortable, but at the end of the day she's a female, and sometimes they are more loyal than your closest homies. I just want her to recognize me as somebody that's straight up and down, because it is what it is. I'd rather hurt her with the naked truth, than a well-dressed lie.

"Well, I see you like Ralph Lauren, what else do you like?"

"Banana Republic, Eddie Bauer, and Guess. You know, the basic brands that don't play out, right?"

"I only asked because we're headed to the mall. Do you need some school clothes, Amin?"

"Hell yeah."

"I got you, baby, just for making me feel like I can deal with you and talk to you. You play cards, Amin?"

"Yeah, I get down."

"Well, you name the game and have it ready for me when I get back."

"Say less."

CHAPTER 3

When Karen leaves out, I gain a clear ear for the next room, Diamond and Damien kickin' it. Minutes later, the conversation disappeared, and then the porn part kicks in. Diamond is moaning all loud and I know freaky ass Damien is loving it, just because he know I can hear it. At the same time, those screams and moans got me harder than an unemployed porn star.

While I'm coming up with a game to play, Karen changed her pajamas and slid into some black, silky fitted shorts, showing off her fantastic figure, the curve of her hips, and her pussy lips.

"So, did you come up with one Amin?"

In a split second I have to get my mind off what I just seen and scrape up a comeback relating to her freaky imagination because why she throw these sexy ass fitted shorts on.

"Yeah...yeah, umm...I figured since I'm a virgin and curious about what it's like, I picked strip poker, since I've never seen a woman in her birthday suit before."

"Amin, damn, hold up…hold up, okay? Just behind the fact you had enough heart to tell me some bullshit like that, we gonna live our lives for a minute. Now put your birthday suit on, or did you bring it?"

I know the facial expression that popped up on my face had me looking dumb as a muthafucka, because she'd caught me off guard with this one. "No, you strip first Karen"

…I guess those moans fuckin' with her too, because as we getting ready to skip the whole poker game and go porn. I'm so nervous my dick shriveled up as if I'd gone swimming or some shit. Damn, my dick small as shit now, but damn now that she's up close and personal with me, her scent is turning me pass on. My no she ain't face popped on as she begins to zipper down my pants, looking back up at me with her pretty ass eyes. Smirking, I thought this only happened when i be imagining shit, would it be this great this fast fo' real?

"Lay on your back, Amin, I'm about to take you on a fantasy ride."

Her sex drive must be in full effect right now. One thing I know is that people do what they wanna do, whenever they wanna do it, and that saves me from looking at her as a freak. Shit, I'm just glad it's me she wanna do the damn thing with.

Karen gets on top of me and eases her way down on this hard ass love muscle. Her face begins to wrinkle, while she's looking directly in my face; she releases the sexiest sound of relief. The ride is no longer wireless, I got a firm grip on her waist, pulling her further down on this muscle. She now lays on top of me as she lets the full freak come out of her. Her love tunnel feels like it was made just for me. Her walls is tight and wet and when I get up in that second hole it's like she passes out for a min but I'm loving every second. She sound so sexy as she whisper in my ear.

"Oooohhh baby, are you enjoying my performance, and how I'm just riding up and down on this dick?"

"Shit! Yes, girl, this pussy so good I promise I duck the next time I promise shit, I'm gonna want more of this."

"Oh, so you're just happy to be in this pussy, Amin?"

"Girl, I kinda like how you say my name, you enjoying your cruise?"

"You silly boy."

Since the ball is in my court now, I'm turning her around about to get deep in her shit I wanna hear everything she has to say but Damn, she's one pretty muthafucka, I think as I grab a fistful of her hair. My nosey ass is busy watching how my dick looks as I'm thrusting in and out of her.

I guess Karen said fuck being quiet, because she's cumming, and screaming like nobody's here with us. Just as she's heatin' up, I'm about to lose control and spend it all on this back shot. My firm grip in her hair is getting tighter.

"Bitch, you fucking the right nigga now, because this pussy is mine, you hear me?"

"Yes...yes...yes...oooohhhh, sssshhhiiittt...You feel so good!"

I haven't had sex in so long, till the point when I busted a nut, my knees went out, and I straight fell on her. To add to that embarrassing moment, Diamond come flying in the room, and caught me while I was outta gas breathing hard, cheeks all out laying on Karen's back, fuck it she got me.

"Oh shit, Karen, you okay?"

"Diamond, can you give us a minute please?"

"Okay. Shit, I had to check because damn, y'all loud in here., all falling and shit...hmm must be nice, now get up; you know we gotta get ready to hit the mall." "But it was okay when you was in there sounding like you found the best fuck in the United States Of America tho', It's okay, here I come, let me get my shit together."

As Diamond closes the door, I hear Damien laughing and screaming, "Oh okay, Amin, that's right, homie."

"He's crazy, Karen."

"You wanna hit the mall with us, Amin because we about to leave now and school lets out at three and shit you don't want your mom catching you half stepping between school hours?"

"Fuck it, why not Karen? It ain't like I'm going to school."

"That's cool, but just so you know, we ain't buying shit."

"Shit, now I do."

"I was going for me, but now I'm going for us. I think I like you, Amin."

"I think I like you too, Karen. You just fucked me like you missed me."

"Don't start talking shit now, but you do have a nice shot. Your handsome face and your sexy demeanor just made me wanna unbuckle your pants and suck on the head for a minute."

"Shit, you just gave me a second wind. My knees back up and running now, come here."

"Chill, that's to be continued; we gotta go steal you a new look."

Damn, she don't even know me and ready to go steal for me. I wonder if people see more in me than I do?

"So Karen, what brings you here? I don't remember seeing you in the hood."

"Yeah, I know. My boyfriend got killed over some dope money out West Philly and his sister's feeling like I set him up, all because I caught him cheating on me, these niggas kidnapped him that same night. His sister burned my house down on some dead wrong shit. Fuck that nigga; the bitch I caught him with is the same hoe I told him I couldn't stand. Then come to find out, he was taking care the hoe! Shit, it broke my fucking heart when I caught 'em kissing in the Chinese joint I had the taste for some Shrimp & Broccoli, i seen that shit I wanted to bite his muthaphukin ass."

"Whoa…Karen, like damn, can it be me to put the smiles back on your face and the happiness back in your heart?"

"Can you maintain all this special romantic shit you saying?"

"Can you keep me feeling like the greatest man alive?"
"Amin, you became him after I fucked you, so now what?"

"Okay then, well, let's give it some time to get to know each other more."

"Okay Amin, I got you, but one thing you need to know is that I'm attracted to your personality, and when I love, I love deep. I don't mean to scare you with the love word, but I know it's gonna happen soon."

"Yeah, I hear you. Just relax, let's take some walks in the park together. You know, beginner's love type of shit."

"You must not have a girlfriend, huh?"

"No, but you picked a fine time to ask."

"No nigga, even if you did, your performance in this pussy told me you was leaving that hoe anyway."

"So what's this, love at first sight, Karen?"

"Don't it feel like it?"

"I feel like a nut, but I like you."

Diamond suddenly screamed through the door, "Yo Karen, are you decent?"

"Yeah Diamond, we descent, are y'all ready?"

"Yes Bring that .357 with you, Karen."

As I'm getting dressed, I overhear Damien talking to Diamond. "Aye Diamond, Amin must've got a hold to that ass good, this bitch got manners now. What kinda shit is that? Fuck a bitch, then change a bitch?"

"You don't need to bring your gun, Diamond," Karen tried to convince her.

"I think I do, Karen, because if any bitch comes at you about that dumb shit, that's when somebody's gonna need a fuckin' doctor. I've told you he wasn't shit, but I guess love is a muthafucka."

"What's up, Amin? You good, big homie?"

"Yeah, I'm good, my nigga."

"That's what's up. Did Karen talk to you about this trip, yo?"

"Yeah, we out. Fuck it."

Damn, I think, seeing these females dressed is almost like meeting them all over again.

When I think about our neighborhood, it kinda gives me an idea of what Las Vegas would be like, because our strip is laced with gamblers, dressed to impress, with fast money and drama. 29th and Jefferson is attractive. Even the dustiest niggas look good to the outside looking in.

As we're leaving, Diamond hits the remote, unlocking the doors to a burgundy, stick shift, Ford Mustang 5.0; I'm impressed, because these cars are fast as shit.

"Karen, are you riding shotgun or Damien?"

"No. Damien, you get up front; I wanna be next to my new boo."

"Damn Karen, you only knew him for twenty minutes."

"Damien, mind your business, and Diamond, can you not drive like a runaway slave please, with this small ass back seat?"

"Don't start that scary shit, Karen, because you ain't say shit when I get to your rescue on time."

"You damn right, my fuckin' girl."

While I'm sitting back enjoying the vibe, I can tell Karen and Diamond are tight for real and I can tell that neither one of them are holding punches about new recruits, especially when you're not welcome, so maybe I should give myself more credit than I do. But damn, this Diamond bitch must be a gangsta bitch. She cuts the radio on and 2Pac's "Me Against the World" starts bumpin' from the four 12" EV's in the back with that bass that vibrates everything in your chest and the high's that's so crispy.

Chapter 4
THE OXFORD MALL

"Okay, y'all just sit here and we will be right back with the goodies."

"Alright, y'all be careful," Damien responded.

"Thanks, Damien."

As the girls left, Damien turned to me, and asked, "So Amin, what happened in that room, nigga?"

"I was treated like a king, you know, like she missed me or some shit."

"Damn yo, you serious?"

"Hell yeah. Shit yo, Diamond has the keys! What if something goes wrong?"

"Relax Amin, I got me a pretty gangsta bitch, but sometimes she makes me nervous. This bitch will shoot anybody...anywhere, anytime. She's money hungry and crazy."

After hearing that, I'm kinda looking at Diamond from a different angle. I'm thinking everything that looks good ain't always good.

"Amin, you smoke weed, my nigga?"

"Naw, I'm good. I need all my brain cells."

"It don't do shit but lean you back, and relax you and bless you with the munchies."

"Yeah, Damien, and who gonna bless me with some munchies money?"

"That's what's real. Stay smart, my nigga, because everybody don't know when to put it out, and then they become somebody you hate to see coming. That's why I like you, Amin, you know when to fold 'em, even though we still kids basically, yo. If my mom and dad wasn't drug dealers, my nigga, we'd probably have more similar situations to conversate about. The most important thing that's more valuable than the money is your mind, you keep making the best decisions for yourself and have some patience Amin shit don't always stay the same."

"So you always smoke that shit and then drop knowledge?"

"Amin, you funny as shit!"

He's right about what he said, because it's amazing how often you can be tested on a daily basis, which is the birth of respect or neglect.

"But you're right, Amin, we need those keys; you've put butterflies in my gut.

Go get them keys for me, Amin."

Before I can make it through the second set of double doors, I see Diamond and Karen coming towards me, loaded with bags.

"Hey Amin, you come to join us?"

"No, we need the keys, Diamond."

"Oh okay, my bad; I'm just tryna get through this part here."

"Here Amin, this bag is yours."

"All mine?"

"Well thanks, Karen. Well appreciated."

"You're welcome. Diamond, give him the keys so we can get back at it."

"Damn, I almost forgot that fast. Here you go, Amin."

"Okay, good looking out, Diamond."

As I turn around, headed back towards the car, I'm feeling special already, curious of what's in these bags, looking at Damien with all this eyeball sign language. "Amin, don't go looking through them bags yet; they about to fill this whole back seat up, so just trunk the bags to keep room in the car."

This is crazy, forty-five minutes have passed by and I've already made five trips taking bags from them but this supposed to be the last trip.

"See, this the only thing I can't stand about this bitch, Amin. She always in some nigga face, laughing and joking, that's why I don't believe in love. I believe in fucking a bitch until I get tired of her ass."

When I zoom into what Damien is talking about, I see Karen calling us over as they talk to these armored truck employees in front of the mall with more bags in their hands.

"Come on, Damo, let's see what they want."

When we get to the girls, they just pass the bags off.

"Damo, can you warm the car up please?"

"Warm the car up? Diamond, come the fuck on."
Damien's jealousy is written all over his face. Before we can get in our seats good, I heard two gunshots and when I look up, I see one of the armor truck employees falling face-first to the ground.

My heart felt as like it came to a thundering stop.

"Damien, these bitches robbing them!"

At full throttle, Karen and Diamond races to the car, customers are frantically running and screaming, trying to get out of the area.

"Damn Amin, I told you she was a lil crazy, my bad, homie! I didn't see this one coming, this the first time she ever did some shit like this!" Back behind the wheel, Diamond drives like a NASCAR chick.

"Damn baby, what the fuck was that about?"

"Not right now, Damien, I need my concentration."

Amin, you okay?"

"Yeah, I'm good."

"Karen, get on point." Diamond dramatically rolls her eyes after she checks Karen.

"Bitch, you just drive this muthafucka, because I like how you just do shit without telling me first, Diamond." "I'm sorry, y'all, I'm just trying to get out my mom's house. I'm tired of hearing her scream to God every time she gets a dick in her, shit. Sometimes she gets mad and put me out altogether."

Karen turns around, and looks in my eyes as we ease past 120 mph on I-95 and says, "Everything is okay."

"Baby, is them money bags heavy?"

"Aye, Damien, what part of leaving me the fuck alone
don't you understand? Let's get away first, nigga."

I'm in the backseat, hoping to God that this is just a dream.
I've only seen shit like this in the movies, but Karen just
grabbed me by my balls and told me to keep
'em big, that was my confirmation—this is not a dream,
and i know a wise man once said it's always a price to pay
when you play but damn.

CHAPTER 5

Before we knew it, we were back at Diamond's house and got the same parking spot. Diamond and her mom live on Newkirk Street off Jefferson, where it's pretty laidback and peaceful. I kinda like this block.

"Okay y'all, let's move. Bring those clothes, take all the tags off them, and then take it all to the trash that's on the corner of this block, not in my trash."

When Diamond dumped the money on her mother's living room floor, I damn near pissed on myself. I never saw so much money up close and personal in my life, only on TV. I checked everyone else's facial expressions and everybody looks the same. Before Diamond's mother or any other relatives show up, Diamond has us do everything as quick as possible. When we were done counting, the end count was 300,000 dollars, leaving us 75,000 apiece. Diamond hands me my cut.

"What is this for, Diamond?"

"Amin, that's yours. Shit, you might as well get an even cut, because you're just as guilty as I am and again, I'm sorry.

It's just this muthafucka was all smiling because I responded to his flirt. But when I turned him down, he started talkin' about some, 'Fuck you then, I know you wish you had some of this paper don't you, you broke bitch'? When he said that, I knew i was taking all that shit So take this money and put it up, and please don't go tell everybody Amin I'm serious"

"No doubt and thanks, Diamond, I wasn't expecting all this, but shit, Dee, can I take a shower and get cute on these muthafuckas?"

"Oh, I'm Dee again. Fuck it, Amin. Call me whatever, but go ahead and get cute, my nigga."

"Aye, Damien i don't think I'm going be able to figure this one out, he want to be cute at a time like this."

"A Diamond you might've caught us off guard with this shit but we don't give a fuck, it is what it is."

While I'm in the shower, I can hear a new voice downstairs. I wonder whom it belongs to. Quickly, I dry off and slid into a blue RUN-DMC sweat suit with the white stripes. If that's her mom downstairs, I hope Diamond told her I was up here playing water sports.

When I'm finally on my way downstairs, I come into the view of another drop dead gorgeous woman, and I guess this is Diamond's mother, looking like her twin, wearing a red fitted dress, and nice white high heels. Sheesh, she has a nice ass on her.

"And your name is?"

"Mom, this is Karen's friend, Amin. His mom ain't home yet, so he asked me could he take a shower, since he spilled a bowl of chili all over him."

"Amin did you ask me to use my H20?"

I'm stuck, and shift from one foot to the other awkwardly, not knowing what else to say.

"Sike, my name is Angel, Diamond's mom and you're welcome."

"Thank you, Ms. Angel."

"Don't call me Ms."

"Oh, my bad, Angel."

"Diamond, why is your boyfriend sleeping on my furniture?"

"Wow Mom, I didn't even know he was out over there."

"Well, he might as well stay sleep for now. I'm about to cook some collard greens, steak, fish, and mashed potatoes."

"Mom, you think we got enough time to run to the phone store real quick and get back?"

"Yeah, just don't have me do all this for nothing."

Diamond reconsiders. "Matter fact, Karen and Amin can go and I'll stay here."

"Well, come on, Amin, let's go before these stores close."

"Let's ride."

This little bit of time Karen and I spent together has created something that's feeling good in me, but at the same time I'm feeling like I just got pimped by the devil. "So Amin, how you feel about what you saw today?"

"I didn't see none of that coming. It basically took me by surprise."

"I asked, because when I looked in your eyes on the ride back, I just saw a blank look."

"Hell yeah that shit is replaying in my head like the way he just fell straight on his face, i felt that shit in my face."

"Oh well, we got away, so fuck it. We got good money and whatever the future holds about this shit just grip that shit and put it in your pocket because the damage is done

"I hear you."

"You hear me, but do you see me? You act like you're afraid to look at me, Amin. Let me find out you shy, nigga."

"It's not that. It's just a form of me having my guards up, because you're so beautiful. I feel like if you touched me one more time, I may want more than a friendship from you, Karen."

"Amin this so don't feel real, I never moved this fast with nobody but when you make somebody feel the way you made me feel then you probably can pull any chick, and it's something in me that don't want to let go of you, makes me want to keep you around, because you tell it like it is. As for me, baby, I been lied to so much and that hurts. I'm a good girl that only accepts pure and real dudes nowadays. I don't fall for the cars, clothes and sharp haircuts. You know niggas be needing all that to impress, not knowing personality is the pimp and for the record, a nigga can be broke but if he fucking retarded at the same time then i know right there he's never going nowhere."

"Yeah. Shit, I dress accordingly to the weather. In my book, it's best to be straight up and down about things. Lying is a job that I won't ever get paid for, i definitely got dreams baby."

In the blink of an eye I'm taken off guard and i find myself slammed up against the poppy store wall with Karen's tongue down my throat, something I was imagining doing to her while I wasn't catching eye contact.

And fuck who's paying attention, I let her feel the truth from my tongue to let her know I'm falling too.

"Okay Amin, I see you're a kisser, but damn, I don't mean to sound fast, but I wonder why I'm not ready for you to separate from me yet. Like, I'm falling in love with you. It feels like it's something in you that belongs to me on some real shit."

"I got the same feedback and i believe you because you said it in two different ways, but I didn't wanna sound like something, while you wasn't feeling nothing. It's strange to me too. It feels good also. So, where do we go from here?"

"We gonna get these cell phones before Center City shut down. Then when we get back, I'm gonna get Diamond's mom to get us a hotel room at the Four Seasons for a week. I let you run down my leg so that moment can last a little longer, but it dried too fast so we got some unfinished business buddy."

CHAPTER 6

Back at the house, we walked in and Ms. Angel got it smelling good. I've never been happier in my life. Today I woke up, bumped into a dream chick, became a sucker for love and came up on seventy-five G's. What's fucking with that?

"What's up, Damo? You up now, nigga?"

"Yeah, I was tired, been up all night. My dad had me clean the basement, backyard and the bathroom. He be on some dumb shit sometimes."

"Shit, at least he around."

"Amin, he be on some 'tryna prove a point' shit."

As we wait for the collard greens to get done, time marches into 5:00 pm. Up next, breaking news shows up on this nice 72-inch Samsung flat screen that's on Diamond's wall, representing a robbery homicide that took place at the Oxford Mall. I glance at Damo and he's glued to the TV, while the ladies conversate in the kitchen. Now all of a sudden, I gotta take a mean shit, my heart is skipping beats and my hands are beginning to sweat. I wonder where the remote control is, so I can turn it, but I know I need to see this shit at the same time.

The collard greens are done and now we're all gathering at the table to eat. I've lost my appetite, but I'm gonna eat anyway, they do things that normal functional families do.

They pray and represent appreciation for a hot meal before they eat, and I respect that.

"Amen."

Now that everybody's at the same place, same time, they're back on the robbery homicide for breaking news. This time, all of us are glued to the TV. Diamond's mom was in the middle of her speech, but got distracted by Diamond & Karen's facial expressions as they stare at the news. The more we watch, the sadder things become. The surveillance cameras from the mall's parking lot had captured every move. They zoomed in on all of our faces for a clear visual. Then they kept showing Diamond blow this guy's brains out, to make her look extremely dangerous. Out the corner of my eye I'm clocking how Diamond's Mother is trying to keep it together but falls to her knees and burst into uncontrollable tears.

"What the fuck did you do, baby? What did you do? Oh my God. Lord please, Lord. Oh my God, what did you do?"

My eyes are watering, because i know this outcome is not good. How the fuck did this happen to me? They even have a good visual on the tags.

Damien just pulled his phone off the charger, ready to bail out. As for me, I'm stunned and I don't know what to do.

"Mom, we gotta get outta here. I'm so sorry; I didn't mean to get noticed. Can I use your Mercedes?"

"You dumb bitch! All that shit is in my name! They gonna pull anything in my name until I'm cleared! They want me right now, twin. Once my alibi checks out, then your ass is hot!"

Damien bailed out and me, I'm riding until the wheels fall off. Fuck it; I might as well.

Without a plan B, Karen, Diamond and I jump in a family cab to search Craigslist for private owners with nice cars. Before our taxi could make it off Newkirk Street, there's Damien, turning the corner with a bright idea written all over his face.

"Excuse me sir, can we pick this gentleman up before we proceed?"

The taxi driver pulls up to a stop, and looks nervous as Damien enters.

"Nigga, I thought you was bailing out on me."

"Diamond, you know I won't ever do nothing like that. What I got for you is my mom's Range Rover. I threw twenty thousand at her and she bit, because she knows our situation. She ain't gonna do no funny shit like report it stolen or nothing, so take these keys and be careful."

"But why it sound like you not coming?"

"Probably because I'm not."

"What? I can't believe it, Damien."

"Okay, okay, fuck it. I'll be around there. Diamond, calm down. Take this shit how it come while we still on the street."

"Karen, this muthafucka got me hot, but didn't he just say he wouldn't bail out on me?"

"Okay, on to the next, get the Range and it's on you, Amin."

"Fuck it; we head down south to my folks in South Carolina. They miss me anyway and shit, we just gotta get it how we live from here."

"Baby, I heard how you spoke to the driver, you sounded so educated."

"Karen, I rather sound like a college student than a street thug any day in front of the unknown. Keep that in mind."

When we got around to Damien's house on 30th, between Master and Jefferson Streets, we came across a pearl white Range Rover.

"Here's fifty dollars. Thank you and for future reference, can I have your personal card?" Karen asked.

"Yes ma'am," the driver agreed.

I see Karen is not only gorgeous; she's a thinker.

"Okay, so now what, Damien?"

"Baby, we have to split up."

"But Mr. Asshole, we all from the same hood. You're not safe in Philly ever again, so okay, are you coming or what?" Diamond had an obvious attitude.

"Naw baby, I will call you."

"Aye, Damien, if your mom's truck comes back stolen, I'm taking you the fuck outta here, you heard me, nigga?"

"Aye Dee, don't talk to me like that."

"Muthafucka, I will kill your ass like right now."

Diamond is fast on the draw; she's got her .357 aimed directly in Damien's face.

"We fall under pressure and now you wanna split up?"

"Baby, chill out. I'm just fucking scared."

"I can't tell. You acting like we ain't shook, nigga., Man fuck this nigga; we out, I don't feel secure for his safety down there, nigga just wanna show off, that's it."

"Okay Amin, where do we go from here?"

"Shit, we can't jump on the road right now, because shit just might be blocked off with checkpoints looking for people that look like us. So we gotta go somewhere to chill and cool off a lil bit."

"Makes sense, baby. Every decision we make gotta be above the law; anything less is pushing it," Karen adds.

Karen sounds so sexy when she's serious. Meanwhile, I guess we gotta find a hotel. I wonder how this this gonna go without Damien. Twenty minutes on I-76 and I'm all in the sky. The sun is going down and the clouds are plain and mild. Diamond has her Versace glasses on, as her pretty hair blows back. Karen threw her hair in a ponytail, adding a bang to the front for a much younger look. In the meantime, I'm sittin' here feeling like an actor, starring in my own kind of movie.

CHAPTER 7

THE RADISSON PLAZA

We landed safely in a good hotel downtown, thanks to the offer from a couple of drug addicts that I guess ran outta money. They sold us one night for fifty dollars. I had them go get us an extra week, as long as we can keep it in their name. Damn, it's already a plus that we're in downtown Center City, but wow, I never knew the inside of the Radisson Plaza looked like it's built for Donald Trump. It has a huge gym. It even has a wedding hall, sheesh. Now that we're at the bedroom, I'm amazed. There are two king sized beds, everything is roomy, cozy, and warm; it's very welcoming. The most I could do is sit here and look dumb for a minute. This joint has a bar in it, and a store. It goes on and on; I think I wanna move in this joint. While I'm acting all neat, folding my Polo outfits, I notice these two just jumped in two different showers. Damn, I'm feeling shy again, because I know ain't no shame in their game. I already saw the Victoria's Secret stash. I eased over to the window and oh my God, I can't believe this breathtaking view; I can see everything.

Taken by surprise, my new cell phone rings. "Hello."
"Yo, who is this?"

"This Amin, who is this?"

"This Damien, yo, they just grabbed Diamond's mom on some disrespectful shit. My lil cousin just came and told me they brought her out the house in her panties and in handcuffs, yo."

"They who?"

"DEA, nigga."

"Oh shit, I'll get back." Now our time is limited, but I bet I won't be the first to fuck this moment up. I see Karen slide out the bathroom in something red and sexy and ease under them thick ass comforters. I can't choke up now. I gotta fuck around and take over.

"Amin, are you okay?"

"Yeah, I'm good."

"Why you way over there then?"

"Just allowing the day to catch up with me as I enjoy this view."

"Well, what part of the day got to you already?"

"The part when you sank those manicured nails in my back, as you released the sexiest moans, while I went deeper and deeper."

"I was hoping you had the right memories over there and damn boy, either you went to school for that shit, or you just got a mean ass sex game. When you started hitting this G-spot, it seemed like my brain started sending all the wrong messages through my body. You made me feel so good."

"Well Karen, for the record, I never had pussy that put the dumb look on my face before. I can't forget how that pretty face wrinkled up while you were looking right at me. Damn, that got me fucked up. Then the sound effects alone will make a nigga explode."

Now here's Diamond. The beginning of a complicated night and that's only if I'm talking too fast, because I don't know how they really get down. Shit, this girl just walked past me in the sexiest two-piece in the business. I hear a Cell Phone ringing and I already know it might be Damien calling to fuck this whole thing up.

"Karen, is this your phone ringing or mines?"

"That gotta be yours, Diamond. My shit still in plastic."

"Oh okay. Hello. What... why you calling my phone, chump? Are you serious, Damien? Oh my fucking goodness... What? Oh no the fuck you didn't just say come and get you, nigga, we shot. We separated when you decided not to come! Fuck you!"

Diamond hung up the phone, and turned to Karen. "Damn Karen, they locked my mom up.

I know she's going through it right now. What should I do? I need some fucking help. Damn, all this shit is my fault!"

"Wait a minute, Dee, don't come down too hard on yourself, because none of us prayed for this part. Besides, your mom's alibi has nowhere else to go but to check out. This is our shit, thanks to you, Ms. Mad Ass."

"I guess one apology is too many and a million ain't enough for this, but the damage is done, so what the fuck."

"Hold up y'all," I interrupted. "For one, y'all too loud and two, ain't no good decisions gonna be made from a mad mind, so calm down and let's enjoy this night. Shit, our time is ticking."

"Damn Karen, he just bust out with some knowledge, huh? Ha, just joking, Amin."

As the night begins to settle in, I realize while I'm in the shower, I don't have any underclothes so umm... I guess I'll stroll out this sum-bitch on my boss, walk on some butt naked shit then ask where the snacks at. But as much as I'm trying to water down how this shit got me feeling, the more reality is settling in.

"Aye Karen, check this out. You know how I'm feeling right now? I'm fucking upside down right now. I need a million memories to sit on this situation."

"And Diamond you're saying this to me because?"

"Can we share Amin tonight?"

When I turn around to look at Karen, I have to hold my laugh in with everything I got, because Karen looks like she's just seen a ghost.

"Oh yeah, baby, you're going through it and that's beginning to bother me."

"Why, because I gave a power question?" At least I asked."

"No, you've changed already; you're just not the same., You basically just volunteered Amin's services. How you know if he's stingy with it or not?"

"Damn, you're right. Fuck it, I'm gonna turn it down some."

While they go through that, I hop in the bed where Karen is and start munching on some Oreo cookies as I'm wiggling twinkling my toes.

"Well, Amin, how you feel about being double-teamed?"

"Shit, it's whatever. Just don't hurt nothing. If this is gonna make her feel better, Karen, then how you feel about me being double-teamed?"

A moment of silence crept in the room. I'm nervous, because this is my first time having two girls, two bad muthafuckas at that.

"So Diamond, what are you gonna do with Damien?"

"I don't know, because that money got him thinking retarded. but fuck that, he supposed to be right here."

"Well, it is what it is then. It's no looking back, Diamond."

"I hear you, Karen. Damn, I lost the lust for the fun. Fuck, y'all can fuck on like I'm not here."

"It's nothing like a good friendship. It's so priceless and welcoming; the feeling just keeps you moving right along."

Quietly, the next morning awakened us with the birds chirping, a good beam of sunshine coming through the white blinds. I don't remember, but I think I fell out first. I have to get us outta Philadelphia without getting bagged. I know Mom is worried half to death and after I tell her I'm on the run for murder, she'll probably piss right there, while she's on the phone. I always did hate hurting my mom, but she needs relief. I'm sitting here, looking ten-carat stupid as I ring my mom's phone.

"Hello, Mom?"

"Yeah boy. Where the hell you been? The police are looking for you for questioning about a robbery homicide. Oh, and ya boy Damien, just got killed by the police as soon as I came from out of Cut-Rates. My God, what did y'all do Amin? You robbing shit now?"

"No Ma, this all caught me by surprise. I signed up for none of the above."

My conversation alarmed the girls, mainly about Damien's murder. I didn't realize how loud I was talking. Now we all on the phones. Fuck we all hot now, so there's no room for making scary moves. We outta here; looks like we're headed down to the dirty-dirty. While Karen and Diamond are on the phone, I'm calling my folks in South Carolina to remix the reason for our arrival. It's time to go now, I get up dick swinging east, south just everywhere then I'm taken by surprise from our hotel room door being kicked open, and now all I see is badges and big guns being aimed at us.

"If one of you muthafuckas move, I promise I won't stop shooting until it's time to reload."

Out the corner of my eye, I can see Diamond's hand reaching slowly under her pillow. I think I'm about to fart. Shit, I hope it's only air. I feel like I'm two breaths away from a heart attack. My heart is beating faster than a muthafucka. All I'm left to do is remain silent as they analyze our facial features, sizing us up against the pictures they have in their hands.

"Where is Bakia Simmons?"

We all just gave a fast look at each other. Then outta nowhere, the female officer smacks Diamond with everything she had. "Bitch, can you hear? Where the fuck is Bakia?"

"Bitch, my name ain't Bakia; fuck you and Bakia. You can take that badge off and we can rip that shit, ho. Put your fucking hands on me again."

Damn, it's nearly fifteen ATF agents piling in here, but damn, who the fuck is Bakia? I decide to intervene.

"Um, excuse me sir, ma'am, to cut your investigation in half, on our way in here to get a room, we were stopped by a couple advertising a good room for dirt cheap. We only took advantage of a good opportunity."

Suddenly, one of the agents says, "We clear, we apologize for the inconvenience. Bakia Simmons still has this room, according to the front desk, so this is where we come to. When you see her, you call me at this number. We want that bitch bad. She stabbed her three-year-old son to death because he wouldn't go to sleep, you gonna see it on the news anyway. Come on guys, let's roll."

I never saw people look so good when they leave. Damn, they look good as hell, better than they did when they came in. After the door shuts, my mind is racing. Shit, what the fuck was that? Diamond and Karen wanted to have some fun, so fuck it, it's on.

CHAPTER 8

I walk over to Diamond, while she sits on the edge of the bed. I grab a handful of her hair on some aggressive shit.

"Open your fuckin' mouth."

With ease, she cooperates. I stand on my tippy toes, and filled that fast ass mouth up with a hard dick. I'm only doing this, because she just made me mad as hell; she could've had us taken down to the station for all that gangsta shit she said. But damn, she really deep throating, and but I'm feeling how she can just rock out in front of Karen.

"Come here, Karen, I think she need some help over here."

I lay on the bed and watched as Karen beat Diamond to this love muscle. Looking me in the face, she does tongue tricks all around the belly of this dick. Diamond finds her place by gently placing both nuts in her mouth with the sexy sound effects. I so can't believe my eyes right now. I've only daydreamed about this shit. I grab Karen's hair and let her know I need all this dick in her mouth, and she goes for the gusto. I think these mixed bitches love aggression.

I gotta get Karen off me. She got me ready to spray all this DNA in her mouth and it just can't happen like that. I gotta fuck Diamond while I can get away with it. "Diamond, get on your knees and poke that ass out for me." I like to watch the whole transaction. Oh shit, when Diamond bent that ass out, putting all her privacy on display, my knees damn near went out. This bitch looks good.

I can't do but so much when it comes to affection, behind the fact that I just don't know how much rope Karen gave me. I'm grabbing her by the waist, slowly easing deeper and deeper. I'm eye hustling as she gripping the sheets tighter and tighter. I'm also keeping an eye on Karen, in case she decides she ain't with it no more.

This girl is so fucking tight, damn, this is getting ready to be fun. I'm about to trash her.

Outta patience from working my way in; I'm halfway in, so I pick up speed. Now, bouncing her lil pretty spread out ass on this dick, I can feel me going into that second hole in the back of the pussy. She probably used to sing in a choir, because she's loud as hell. Now the game plan is to make her bust a nut first, so when I get to fucking Karen, she will be able to feel my sexual attraction didn't change. I'm going to drive her ass nuts in just a second.

"Umm...umm...umm...oh my God. Oh Amin...Amin. Ohhh, shit, fuck oh my God! Ahhh, shit fuck me! Ohhh shit, Amin, I'm cumming!"

This girl done pulled one whole side of the sheets off the bed. This pussy is amazing. I just couldn't bust though, not in Diamond. Fuck it; I just pulled out, grabbed Karen's legs, threw them in the air and started licking her belly button, French kissing it, inching closer and closer down to her love tunnel. My tongue finally lands on that spot, and boy, her moans are so fucking sexy, she'll probably make me explode before I even get in her...sike.

When I lifted up off Karen, I notice her eyes are watery. Yes! I got her ass too. I'm skipping the "Why you crying question" because oh shit, she feels good. She locks her arms around my neck, pulling me into a kiss. Now I gotta put my cheeks in it; when you put them butt cheeks in it, it's no longer just a fuck. She's actually crying, tryna hold it back. I can't hold this shit, and I can feel it coming, just as I'm feeling her nails sink into my neck.

"Amin baby, please don't leave me. I been so hurt by men and I'm so happy and comfortable with you. I will do anything to keep you satisfied. I promise."

She just stole my heart with that one, because her tone of voice was just so sincere. I actually believe her; in fact, I never had a woman sound so sexy when they want me to know something.

One side of my face is damn near soaked from sweat, and from her tears. She just touched my heart with that shaky voice.

Karen takes her arms away from my neck and grabs two handfuls of her hair turning side to side; looking at her wrinkled facial expressions is turning me helpless. I'm about to blow. I aggressively grab her face so she can look in my face, "Are you my woman, baby?" "Yes, yes!" she screams, between gasps for air.

"No bitch, is you gonna act like it?"

"Amin, I'm cumming. Ohhh, baby, you feel so good. Oh damn, boy, what the fuck! Damn!"

We exploded damn near at the same time. Yeah, this is mine.

"Well, damn. Karen, I wish Damien talked that kind of shit to a bitch, that type of talk make a bitch act right," Diamond snapped, sounding jealous as hell.

"Diamond, don't start your shit."

"Karen, this is me. Don't change up now that you getting dick again."

"No Diamond, you changed. Ever since this bullshit hit the fan, you ain't got a bright idea the first. Do you?"

"Karen, I was thinking about calling my dad, give him the scoop, and then get a couple more guns for y'all, as well as his Mercedes."

"Shit, that sounds good. Go ahead and make that call, and I'm gonna call my folks down south to let them know some shit.

I had to scrape up the perfect words before I called because my folks are original and will not hesitate to point out anything generic."

"Yeah Amin, that sounds good. Maybe your folks can rent us a house or know somebody that's renting."

As time moves along slowly, I'm getting broken in to Karen and Diamond's company. We can drift into any memory, but when we get back, this bullshit is still here waiting on all of us. All phone calls been made and everything is good.

The Benz is on its way, as well as two .380 handguns. Diamond loves the .357.

"Amin, you know how to drive?"

"Yeah, I'm advanced. Why you ask?"

"Because we might need to slide a suit and a pair of glasses on you, while you take us to our new home." "Oh, okay, I been thinking too. We need to find some homeless people that look like us, with the same height and get them drunk or high, then clip their ID so if we get stopped, we can get past."

"Wow Karen, you gotta good scheming ass nigga. Shit, that's a good one, but my dad will be here soon and we need to be rolling. I can't believe he's giving me his E-Class wagon. It's all black with cream interior with a nice system in it."

"Well, we don't need to be loud, Diamond."

"I know, Karen, but where's your bright idea?" Diamond retorted.

"If we get pulled over, as soon as the cop walks away from the car, we jump out and kill him. Fuck it; I'm in fuck-it mode," Karen fires back.

"Wow, Karen, I hear you."

"Yeah, we don't have time for a joke now."

"Okay, come on, let's get our shit together. My dad's a speed demon."

"Now I get it; you get it from your dad."

"Yeah girl, I like to fly sometimes. Amin, don't tell me you drive like a turtle."

"No, I just enjoy the ride."

"Amin, how do you feel about this shit we in?"

"It wouldn't make sense to complain. It's all said and done now were fucked."

"Oh well, with that being said, let's be on our way. I know my dad is downstairs ready to call me anyway."

Behind the wheel of a Mercedes Benz makes me feel important and I smirk as I'm speeding at ninety miles per hour around the curve on I-95.

Watching out the side of my eye, I can see Karen is laid back in the passenger seat as we listen to The Lox. We're on our way down south, the fucking dirty-dirty.

As I burn this highway up in silent mode, I notice how this situation is changing me; it's making me aggressively bold, I'm starting to feel fuck it-ish.

"My baby on some balla shit. He can handle it at these speeds around these curves. Bitch what?"

"Oh, he's your baby now?"

"Yeah, he was your baby too, especially when he just walked up to you and shoved his dick in your mouth, bitch. Think before you start talking shit."

"That's all I'm doing, bitch. Calm down, I'm not gonna take your man. Damn, Amin, she makes you sound easy."

"No, both of y'all sound easy, because y'all on some other shit. Like the shit on our plate ain't serious."

"Wow, Karen, I guess we can call him power lines. He always gotta nice bar to spit, but be on some real shit. Thanks Amin, but you do know that we just joking, right?"

"Whatever, Diamond," I answer her, paying her no attention."

EIGHT HOURS LATER

Pulling up in my grandfather's driveway, I notice all of my family is here waiting for my arrival, but they're gonna be shocked when I jump out this Benz with my friends. My grand-pop is first to approach.

"Oh my Lord, look at my boy, gotten big and wow driving a Mercedes Benz. Boy, look at you. How you been?"

"I been good, just tryna make it." A warm welcome overwhelms me with all the real and beautiful smiles from my family. I didn't expect a cookout with drinks.

"Hey y'all, I have two good friends with me. This is Karen and Diamond."

"Welcome. Come on in the back so we can break the ice."

Looking around, I feel relieved. I guess when you're beautiful; it's easy for people to accept you, because my aunts are already making small talk and jokes with Karen and Diamond. Everything is good, I'm thinking as I look at my girls, shit, I'm 'bout due for another threesome. I've put a couple of mixed drinks in me and I'm talking shit. A nice time is what it is. A photoshoot just kicked off, and we're all posing and looking good.

"Amin, you have a very nice family down here."

"Thanks, Karen."

"They miss you like you lived down here before."

"Yeah, at one time I did, but it's too quiet for me. I need to be where the action is."

"Well, you damn sure found it."

"Okay, let's finish up today. We can get back to what's real tomorrow."

"Yeah, how about that."

My dad pulls up behind us in the driveway in a late model, pearl white Jaguar, looking famous. Meanwhile, he was telling us sad, broken down stories like everything was going wrong in his life. Shit, we might not be able to stay here too long.

"Amin, what's going on and who are these beautiful women you have here?"

"Damn, you come up like I just seen you last night or last week. What's up with you and where you get the Jaguar?"

This bitch ass nigga started showing off on some bragging shit, trying to impress Diamond and Karen, but making me feel like shit in the process. He hid his wealth like we was out to get him, I can't help but think.

I would kill this nigga if it wouldn't leave us looking like prime suspects. I can practically read Karen's mind, as she looks at my dad with the straight face.

"All this shit he talkin, but your son embarrassed about his clothes, to the point he hooking school. Some parents ain't shit", the look on her face said, while she nodded her head and smiled. The sun goes down, and tomorrow's another day. My aunt is packing up to get ready for work in the morning.

"Baby, it's so good seeing you. Are you staying for a while?"

"Yeah, Auntie Cee. I want to see if I can get accepted in Georgia Tech and that's going to determine how long my stay is going to be."

"Oh okay, well, I'll be seeing you again, I have to go now. Love you and be careful out here."

"I love you too, Auntie." Damn, after telling my aunt some bullshit, I'm hoping my grand pop don't drink too many and tell them all about why I'm here. I don't plan to stay long, but I do miss my folks down here.

After the sun is settled and things became silent, truth and honesty begins to message my thinking. Deep down inside, I know I'm fucked. Tears begin to roll down my face while everyone is asleep. How the fuck did I slide into a fucked-up situation so easily? Why couldn't I see this type of shit coming? Damn, is it meant for me to be fucked up like this?

I hadn't even have any real fun yet, but here I am on the run for the rest of my life.

CHAPTER 9

I really wonder how it is to be dead, because being alive in jail is continuous hell. I don't think I can prep my mind for jail forever. I heard Karen and her thoughts sound the same, but at the same time, I'm not ready for a dead ass conversation either.

"Amin, are you okay over there?"

"Yes Diamond, you scared the shit outta me playing sleep and shit. You okay over there?"

"No...I'm in somebody else's home and I can't sleep. I'm just in my head."

"So I guess Karen ain't sleep either?"

"No, I'm woke, nigga. We saw you over there wiping your tears, you bitch ass nigga."

We all broke out laughing.

"So what, we didn't just steal stuff, we killed somebody."

A door opens and my freaky ass dad walks in wearing his boxers, his rock hard dick showing, with one sock on.

"Amin, did you lock the door?"

"Come on, Dad, you could have come with a better one than that, and you could have put some damn clothes on!"

"Amin, this is my house and I can do what I want here."

Damn this dude has nothing for me; he's showing no love or respect. I should do him a favor and blow his fucking head off, because he still looking at me like, and what? Funny-looking ass nigga; I know why he's alone. He thinks with his dick and these bitches don't want to just fuck, they want to make money, explore their imagination and be entertained. Fuck him! My mom is beautiful and since he left us, she never brought another man into our house, unless he was helping with shopping bags. She could have done her thing before she went shopping, but I admire the respect she kept for me. This dude doesn't know a good woman when he sees one.

"Amin, I'm ready to leave! Damn, how ya pop going to come in here with his boxers on, and one dingy ass sock pulled up to his kneecap though?"

Again, we bust out laughing, and here he comes again.

"Amin, your granddad is asleep. Now if y'all can't keep it down, y'all can get the fuck out."

That did it. I jumped up and whipped out the .40 Glock I got from Diamond. "Muthafucka, let me tell your good for nothing ass something!

Ain't no love in this connection here. I forgave you for going AWOL when I really needed you, but since you have no remorse or respect for me, bitch, you have any last words?"

"So you came to kill your father?" My dad asked.

"Well shit, you ain't give a fuck about seeing me ever again." Diamond gets up and stands in between us.

"No, Amin, come on now, let's just go. Karen, come on, let's go."

"We can't just leave and not know where we're going. Dad, we need you to help us get to a hotel. Can you do this or what?"

"Amin, if you think for one second I'm going somewhere with you, you're crazy. You better call your cousin, Eli."

"Damn, good idea; I need his number."

"I'll be back with it. I will call him first for you."

A moment of silence calmed us for a second as we packed up. Then Dad came back again in those same boxers. What the fuck is wrong with him? "Eli is on his way. He's only a mile away at a gas station, so get ready."

"Okay, we're leaving."

Waiting in the Benz for my cousin, Eli, I'm thinking hard. How am I gonna get outta this shit with no scars? There's no way around this shit.

"Amin, what's the twist with your pop, yo?" Karen asked me, with her face scrunched up.

"Karen, we just learned some shit together, because I don't know that muthafucka."

As we talk, I'm noticing a nice, chromed out motorcycle, downshifting and pulling in near our driveway. This must be Eli. I get out to greet my cousin and all I can say is, "Oohhh, shit! Damn, what's up, cuzzo? What's good, my nigga? Is this how you doing it in the south?"

"You muthafuckin' right; the good life, wish a nigga would life I like to live good, cuz."

Eli is dressed in a cream linen suit, and some burgundy alligator shoes, with a sock around the toe part for the gears.

"Yeah, I just switched up. I had this bike on the back of my pickup truck about to go stunting around the clubs. You know them bitches be out there, even bitches that don't drink, and drug free be on post. They just be baller hunting, you dig me, cuz? But damn, look at you, nice Benz, models, and shit. What's good?"

"Get us a hotel room so we can kick it."

"Oh word, Amin, let's go."

My cousin Eli's always been a handsome, wavy-haired, smooth-talking ass nigga. I already know Diamond might fuck him tonight. No sooner than the thought crossed my mind, Diamond chimed in.

"Damn Karen, I guess his whole family is attractive, huh?"

"So far, everybody been up to date in the face."

"You always be finding new words and shit."

"Girl, shut up!"

"Damn, I need a haircut, or should I cut all this shit off?"

Pulling up in the Hilton, I'm feeling so important in this Benz with my big-time ass cousin. Just listening to Diamond's compliment, confirmed the porn scene and I guess I can't get none tonight from Diamond. I know Eli might want to fuck Karen too, but he sure won't be doing that shit! When we get to the room, there's two king size beds, a Jacuzzi, two walk-in showers, a microwave and a view out of this world. I can look down and see everything from up here on the thirteenth floor.

"Yeah cuz, I'm doing some things. Man, I was wondering when I was gonna see you again."

"Yeah man, just got...Hold up, Eli, I got some serious questions for you before we kick it."

"And what's that, Amin? Come on with the bullshit."

"Have you ever been indicted by the feds?"

"No. Why?"

"Because certain charges by the feds be a job for them to follow you ten, twenty years after you finish parole. Things like money laundering, king pen and organized crime, you dig?"

"Damn, Amin. No, hell naw; I'm good. Shit, but I do have two bricks with me. I was supposed to meet a nigga with them, but they backed down. Now I don't trust them. How you gon' send a nigga to me to talk about buying this shit? I thought we got all that straight, but fuck it."

"Yeah, that's room for some bullshit, Eli. Okay, come on and let me introduce you to my two beautiful women."
"The fuck? You a pimp now?"

"Naw, we just rolling."

"So what brings you down, Amin?"

"I wanna see if I can get in Georgia Tech."

"Oh okay, school boy. Ain't shit wrong with that."

"Ummm excuse me. My name is Diamond and this is my sister, Karen. Pleased to meet you."

"Well, you know my name, I'm Eli."

"Yeah we heard."

"Well, what's up, cousin? It's twelve o clock and the parties are just starting. Y'all in?"

"Shit, why not? Give me a minute to change clothes." I jumped in a cream Ralph Lauren linen set, and then slid into some black Prada shoes Diamond had gotten for Damien. Shit, I guess this the only way I can show respect for his life, because we damn sure can't be at his funeral.

Karen transformed into some black fitted CK1 jeans, patent leather high heels, with a black fitted Versace shirt. Just looking at her makes me wanna sneak and get one off. Diamond came out with a tight white Armani shirt and some all black True Religion jeans with the white stitching. Those jeans were fitting that fat ass just right; fuck around and I'll send Eli to go find his own pussy. Tonight is gonna be a good fucking night.

"Word, we out, y'all. Cuz, do you think I should bring my ICU?"

"Fuck is that, Eli?"

"It's that .40, nigga."

"Shit, I got a MAC-10 so shit, let's get it. Ladies, y'all can warm the car up. We right behind y'all."

"Yes daddy."

"She just made me blush, cuz."

Shit, what kind of life you live, nigga? You got two sisters with you, and don't tell me you didn't sex both of them."

"Yeah, Diamond wanted it to happen, so you know I had to play it off like I really wasn't with it, because the one in them CK1 jeans is my girl."

"Oh, she's notarized, cuz?"

"Yeah, she's notarized, Eli."

"Well shit, I'm in the backseat with Diamond then, cuz. Shit, I'm leaving these two bricks in here until we get back. Word?"

"Word. You still silly, Eli. Talking about some word. You on some throwback Three Times Dope shit."

Back in the Benz, I found Trap Muzik by T.I laying on the floor. The fuck her pop be listening to? He's a hood nigga, probably getting it.

"Turn right and keep straight, cuz. Let me show off the South a lil bit. Shit, it don't start bumpin' until like twelve forty-five anyway."

Damn, the South looks so peaceful. Dirt roads and spaced out houses. I want to stay here and live free. Finally, we're at the club, and I'm at a loss for words, because this joint looks so ghetto. It looks like an alleyway with the houses facing toward you. Jumping out the Benz, I see Eli get more props than a rock star from damn near everybody.

That doesn't surprise me, because he does come from a good family. We are new faces, so all eyes are on us. From the outside, I can hear the DJ in there showing his ass. The dance floor is crowded and everybody is dressed to impress.

"Yo Eli, can I bring my gun in?"

"No, but I got this. The doorman is married to my man's sister."

"Oh okay."

"Damn! Cuz, now check this shit out. Remember I told you about the sale for the two bricks?"

"Yeah."

"Why this nigga over there kicking it with niggas I got squashed beef with? The one in that dirty ass white tee, he was the one who was supposed to come talk about buying something from me."

"Well, make sure I get in with this Glock then, cuz, just in case I have to put a couple in his face, let the blood drip in his drink and give it another taste."

"You silly cuz, but ard."

I put Diamond and Karen on point, and then I said, "Now fuck it, let's have a nice time." Happy as shit, I'm in with my Glock, I ordered a Long Island with a chaser. I really don't want to get drunk too fast.

The DJ just blended some reggae, Sean Paul's "Just Gimme the Light". This joint here just made these chicks put their drinks down and get up to dance. I'm about to bust a move or two, right with this Long Island in my hand.

Soon as I hit the dance floor, there's a chick backing that ass up on me, getting low with it, but I can't do what I want, because my baby in here. After my third drink, I'm ready to go outside. This heat from all these dreadlocks is making me higher. I'm rounding my girls up and I notice that Diamond is drunker than I am. I look towards the door and notice Eli in an argument with somebody outside.

"Excuse me, miss. Can I have a glass of water please?"

"Diamond, snap out of that shit for a minute. We got an issue outside and I need you to be alert, just in case we got to let them thangs blow. Karen, you ready? Shit, bring your drink."

Leaving out the club, I got a closer view of my cousin being surrounded by some aggressive niggas, including this "so-called" middleman.

"Diamond, go start the car and Karen, you stay in the car."

"What? I'm ready to let them thangs go, just like you."

"So what the fuck you saying then, nigga? Wassup?" This

chump's all in my cousin's face.

"Eli, what's up, baby?" I ask my cousin. Eli turns around and I can see fear in his eyes. I'm close enough now to this snake ass middle man. Now here's where it goes down. I grab the middleman and spins him around, so I can have a clear shot at his head.
Boom! Boom!

I put two in his head at close range. "You snake ass nigga," I shout at his lifeless body.

"Oh shit, oh shit, what the fuck? Somebody call an ambulance. Please. Oh my God!" someone screams. Everybody is scattering and now somebody else is shooting, but I can't see who's popping off.

"Eli, come on baby, let's go."

My cousin and I start running towards the car as middleman's brains keeps falling off Eli's shoulders. Fuck a snake ass nigga. Now, I just want to get the fuck outta here. I see a white Caddy speeding down the block, slamming on the brakes, right where we are. Windows begin to roll down and shit, there's the guns.

CHAPTER 10

Karen catches the driver of the Cadillac slippin', taking him out with four facial shots and Diamond is drunk, shooting up everything but our rivals. I'm actually seeing innocent bystanders fall, while I'm unloading my clip through the back window of the Cadillac on some careless shit. I'm beginning to hear ambulance and police sirens, and I'm feeling that we won the war.

I get back to the car and turn around and notice it's just me and Karen. "Where the fuck they at, Karen?"

"Baby they were just right there with us, Amin."

I get back out the car and find Diamond drowning in her own blood, on the opposite side of the car.

"Oh my fucking goodness, Karen, Diamond is dead!"

"Fuck you mean she dead? Where is your cousin at?" I back up to find my cousin Eli face down in the grass.

"Damn Karen, I feel like Eli is dead too. I'm going to check on him."

"Baby, let the ambulance get him; they're too close.

Last thing we need is to be taken down for questioning, now, let's go."

My eyes are blurry as I'm fighting my tears, kind of feeling like my cousin would've never wanted to go to a club if I hadn't come down here.

Before we made it back to the hotel, I went through a Checkers drive thru and as I'm ordering my food, I see a million cops fly pass. Damn, I hope my cousin makes it!

"Damn! Karen, please tell me you got the key."

"You muthafuckin' right; I found it on the bar where Diamond was sitting at. Amin, I feel like your cousin knew something was bound to go wrong, because he left Diamond with the room key."

"Damn Karen, what the fuck? Somebody put a hex on us?"

"Shit it feels like it. First Damien, now Diamond; hopefully, your cousin makes it."

"Yeah, I know, right?" After coming out the drive thru, I'm now wondering how to get back to the hotel. Three hours later

"Amin, don't park in this hotel lot, park around the corner somewhere. Oh and I gotta million-dollar question?"

"What is that?"

"How do I deliver this fucked up message to Diamond's mom, Amin?"

"Karen, how you get this dumb ass look off my face, because after the shit we already in, we damn sure gonna be held responsible. We the last ones breathing, unless Angel just take the story like it is. I think we should just leave without a trace, shit, my dad already don't like me, so I already know he probably threw me straight under the bus."

"Fuck it, Amin, without a trace it is. Love you."

"Love you too."

After I come out of my daze, I remember Eli stashed two kilos of raw in the room.

I scratch my head, thinking, man, what the fuck am I gon' do with this?

Damn, so I'm left with two kilos, three homicides and money. Shit how would I explain my innocence if I get caught with all this on top of the shit we wanted for…sheesh. Diamond looked good in them True Religion jeans, even dead, and Eli was dressed for his own funeral. Damn, this is so fucked up! Now I'm looking at myself in the mirror, and all I see is pain in my eyes. This is not the person my mom wanted me to be, regardless of what she did or didn't do for me, I know she wouldn't want me to be living like this.

"So now what, Amin?"

"We about to take a gamble."

"And that gamble is?"

"We about to jump on the highway with this Benz and hope to God this Benzo ain't on the watch list. Don't get paranoid, just have a Coke and a smile and shut the fuck up."

"You silly and I like the fact that you can joke under this kind of pressure, because I can sense signs of crumble a mile away. You rub me as one of them niggaz that got secret demeanors that ain't for show, until that time calls for it, so it is what it is. I'm glad I met you, because I never felt excited like this about a relationship since my first love."

"So? What the fuck you saying, I remind you of another nigga?"

"No, Amin, this just feels like an emotional orgasm, connected with someone that's about you a hundred percent. Now go ahead and lie, because I can see it in your eyes when you look at me, nigga."

"Karen, I look like I love everybody when I smoke some good shit."

"I guess you want me to bust you upside your fucking head with something."

When I turn to look at Karen, her eyes are watery and her bottom lip is shaking. I better fix this one quick.

"Baby, you know what it is and where my emotions at about you. So why did you just take me that serious?"

"Because baby, I been lied to when I thought it was serious. There's no worse feeling than being notified by somebody's wife that you're the side bitch when you believed everything special a nigga said. Being pretty don't make shit go your way, because if it did, he would've dropped that bitch like a hot potato. I don't mean to blow my own horn, but look at me, and then at this last nigga I was dealing with."

When I turn to look at Karen, she made sure her cute face was on with the blinking eyelashes. We're in the Benz, and I'm driving, pedal to the metal, when Karen says,

"Amin, what the fuck you think, we at the race track or something? Slow down, nigga, you over a hundred miles per hour on a seventy-five." I'd zoned out on a long stretch with this Benz, because this muthafucka float like a canoe at high speeds, so it's easy to forget.

"So Amin, did Diamond suck ya dick better than I do?"

"So, I guess this where the set up begins."

"No pussy, answer my question."

"Well okay, which one you want first, the truth or some bullshit?"

"I want the truth, nigga, why you hesitating about this dick suckin' status?"

I can't help but to burst into laughter, she's got jokes for real. That was just what I needed to break up some of the tension. "So by any chance, if I said something you didn't like, that don't mean I'm gonna get hit with some shit, does it?"

"Just keep it gangsta, Amin, what the fuck!"

"Well, okay… Besides the fact that she was an extra on the porn site, I felt like I could do shit how I wanted to, and the way she had her lips all glossed up…I kinda got a kick out of it."

"Muthafucka, I said, did she do it better than me?" "Well… besides the fact that she was looking up at me, making all them movie noises while she was deep throating with the shiny lips, made her the winner. You didn't get prepared for the event like she did, but before your imagination get lost, just know I don't get good sex mixed up with who I'm in love with. After all, she had your permission to get some of these cookies."

"So, I gotta get prepared for the event now?"

"I'm not gonna lie, baby, that lip-gloss makes the head games feel brand new…like the very first dick suck in the world!"

"Hold up, so that felt like the best dick suck in the world, Amin?"

"Aye Karen, why are you so stuck on this conversation?"

"It's not really about this conversation, Amin. It's an evaluation to determine if we could have a long term relationship and you passed, because I pulled the truth out of you. If you had enough guts to tell me how amazing it was in detail, then I can believe what you say about what you feel about us. I can say that you're believable, because you could've easily downsized the situation, or even said it was a lower level of pleasure. Females are like detectives sometimes, Amin; we can ask you a question about something over east, just to figure out some shit over west by something called unexpected indirect questions. I can tell you what it is, because you won't be prepared for it anyway. Bottom line is this, you keep it real with me, and we're cool."

"Shit you sound like the police."

"Hell no, nigga, you just can't tell me some bullshit and it sinks. I might shake my head like I believe you, but that head shake is to confirm to my own understanding like, 'yeah, that was some bullshit'. Since this topic is hot, tell me why we as people in general, decide to stay in relationships that's not loyal? I ask myself sometimes like damn, is it to see how good of a liar this motherfucker can be, or is it the wait to see if the real eye contact is gonna resurface, along with the laughs and jokes, and that feeling I had when my emotions were comfortable.

So before you decide to council somebody when they dump their problems on you, just listen and understand that if it was a process with you falling in love, it's also a process letting go, and that's only if you wasn't a predictable fuck up. Love is priceless, Amin, but it's everything we live for."

Completely in tune to what Karen is saying to me, it makes my eyes blurry as I'm trying my best to keep it steady in this fast lane. It's true that you don't know a person's story until it's written in a book somewhere. It's also making me think of my mother and what could've distracted her from wanting to do better, Now I feel like I owe her an apology and should let her know I understand what I didn't understand earlier, and to please forgive me for judging her.

"Oh my God, why you crying, baby?"

"Karen, that was the realest shit I ever heard, since the doctor said it's a boy. The conversation just upgraded how I scan people, and I went to reminiscing about me and my mom's relationship. I did notice you do trust me, because not once have you asked me where are we headed."

"Right, where are we headed?'

"I got an aunt in Baltimore, and she about her business in that fast life, meaning like getting rich, and then branching off into selling houses and cars. She been trying to get my mom to move down there with her, but Mom wasn't feeling it."

"But Amin, Baltimore is on fire; it's no different from Philly. These cops be lurking on all kinds of shit and half of them is criminals with a badge."

"Well maybe they'll let us go, if they're the ones who catch us."

"You still got jokes, okay, Amin."

BALTIMORE, MARYLAND

We were supposed to be here in nine hours or so, but I kinda chopped that time in half, balling like a fuckin' boss, because I damn sure feel like one driving this Benz. I love when I can see the curiosity in people when we stop at lights. They're like, "Hmmm, I wonder who they are?" and at that very moment I feel special. When it's time to pull off, I'm back in my rearview and back to reality. I'm coming up on Martin Luther King Boulevard and Lombard Street, and I see Lombard is blocked off with like a million cops and ATF.

"Damn, this where we got to turn at and look what we have here. I see people walking through the block on the sidewalks, so let's park and walk around, or are you scared?"

"No, this just the realest gamble, Amin, but just make sure your Glock is cocked back, and maybe we can blow our way out this shit if we about to get in some dumb shit."

"That's what I like about you, baby; always thinking survival, but come on."

All eyes are on us as we're blending in with pedestrians and the police.

"This might have been a mistake, Karen," I glance sideways, and whisper.

"Just don't give any nervous looks, because you might confuse them and make them come ask us some dumb shit, just to look in our faces. Now, where we going?"

"We going to make this right up Scott Street then come back down Lombard."

When we turn on Lombard Street, the first person I catch eye contact with is my Aunt Rose. They have her cuffed and sitting on the pavement, while the ATF is bringing drugs and guns out her house. She's staring at me like she can't believe it's me, as I'm putting my hands on my head in agreement of disbelief.

"So now what, Amin?"

"Karen, I'm so out of options right now; my aunt was my last move. She rides with me on all angles and I saved her for last, because I know how busy she can be, but by the looks of what they got sitting on top of that cop car and the shit they still bringing out the house, my Aunt Rose gonna fuck around and get life in jail. How you gonna explain two machine guns, along with whatever they got in them bags up there around innocent adolescents? That's probably what's going to kill her, because the're separate charges."

"Wow, was she a loving mother to her kids?"

"Yeah, she overdo it sometimes; I haven't seen her in like five years, but it don't matter, because she gonna always be the same ol' Rose."

"Well, what we can do is take this coke back to Philly and get it cooked up; that's if you want to do that, Amin."

"Shit, we can do that ourselves; we don't need no help for that. Fuck baking soda; we can just have some throwback coke, Karen."

"No, my thing is having this connect help us sell it as well, or he can fuck around and buy this shit."

"Okay, well who is this connect?"

"Like, you know niggas. Fuck outta here, you young chump; you with a big girl that know niggas."

Karen breaks out laughing, and then says, "Sike...no baby, it's this dude, Cargo, that was on my head back in the day, making ten thousand dollar offers to have me in his life. He was homeboys with my ex and he came at me with all that when we was together and I would've done it, if I didn't feel like he would kill my boyfriend. That nigga treated me bad, just because he seen I wasn't going nowhere. Amin, I'm one loyal chick and it seems like niggas get it confused, as if it was the dick that got me loyal.

We suffer the most, the good ones that is. If I was a mystery bitch, I would've had that nigga stalking me, nobody likes that feeling of being cheated on, and I like a challenge at the same time, so yeah, I went through some ol' unnecessary shit before."

I can't escape how good this breeze feels, it's looking like it's about to rain and the scent of wet grass, along with this friendly mild breeze is really showing some affection right now. I'm going to sit here in this parking spot for a second, let the radio play and let some Gerald Levert shit sneak up on me, while I'm appreciating my freedom. This is one of them "lay around the house" days, when you caught the middle of a good movie, off and on snacks, and then the fun part happens. Shit, this breeze about to make me sing some shit.

A MOTHER'S PAIN

When I look back at the day my baby boy, Amin, was born, I guess I was supposed to drop everything that didn't benefit me, and pick up new ways to make a special life for the sake of my son's future. I neglected the fact that this is really a life that I brought into this world, a sense of humor with independency. I wish there was something that made me pay more attention to more detail towards his needs, as far as his comfort and his confidence were concerned, because damn, this is overwhelming. I don't have a clue where he is or if the cops have killed him and left him to be thought as just a victim or what. I just know that if I gave him everything and spoiled him like my sisters do their kids, he probably would have grown up thinking he could live off people.

As the Bible says, "If you spare the rod, you'll spoil the child". I wanted to be sure that if he outlived me, he would be independent, because when a child is young and wants everything his friends have, and doesn't get it, that places the urge in him to want to earn his own money. That creates the birth of independence in that child.

Unfortunately, the untold story about why I couldn't take care of him as I really wanted to, is because I've been a violent felon since way before he was born. I beat homicide cases that left me everlasting enemies. Who the fuck is going to hire me for a good job? I was scared to get pregnant and things didn't work out for this very reason, because I knew his dad wouldn't know or possibly care if he's okay or not.

I knew better, but when a nigga wants you while you're struggling...yeah I turned his father down more than ten times, but one night he rolled up on me when I was thinking about a hustle without the question of selling my ass. I hopped in his Porsche and didn't realize how attractive he was up close. He had wavy hair, a pair of the sexiest eyes, his teeth was bright white, a sign that he's not a drug abuser, with a clean, light- brown skin complexion. I was impressed, but couldn't show it and it seemed as if this nigga just had all the right shit to say. I was scared to look down so his eyes can follow me, because this smooth talking mothafucka had this pussy soaking wet.

It wasn't so much what he was saying to me, it was the way he was looking at me when he was talking. He made me want to get away from him before I disrespected the reason why I wanted him to wait. However, when that time came for us to accidently get into it, this nigga gave me the Superhero dick. I didn't think I could look at somebody so strange during sex, but damn, Rakim must of went to school for that shit.

He gave me thousands of dollars at a time that led me to believe that if we did have a kid, I would have no worries. Sadly, when I did have a child with him, Rakim started dissolving away slowly. but surely, and was completely gone before we could can have the "are we going to be a family" conversation. What I've later learned is that these niggas will say and do anything to get you, but the thought of consistent commitment does something to the way a man looks at you, that's not every man, so don't get it twisted. I wish I'd been really lucky; then my son would be on his way home or upstairs already. I'm hoping we can talk and he'll understand and forgive me for being a victim of circumstance, instead of looking at me as an unfit mom. Shit happens and Lord knows I don't want him to meet any more of the fake ass home boys. I heard about what happened before they showed it on the news, all because his homeboy, Damien, was going around bragging about how he rides and probably didn't do a damn thing. I didn't expect Damien to war with the police at all; that's the reason him and my son became friends; violence brought them together.

ANGEL

I guess I should've stayed my ass over in Puerto Rico where I was, but I was so tired of being there. If I'd stayed, perhaps Diamond would've listened to her father. I just didn't like when he became abusive when she got out of control. In my head, I'd rather go to jail in the United States before I went back to jail there. It seems as if your greatest fears about your child isn't the shit that happens, because I always visualized her being in an abusive relationship, coming home with black eyes behind the fact of how sweet she used to be. As she grew older though, I began to fear for the man who fell in love with her, because my innocent lil Diamond went from the sweetest lil girl to somebody you didn't want to fight with.

When my lights got shut off, my fourteen-year-old Diamond disappeared for a couple days, and then came back with nearly five thousand dollars. Then when I asked her where she got the money, of course she lied, but she told me that she hated the look of worry in my eyes. Tears just ran down my face like a waterfall in disbelief of how much my baby loved me. But come to find out, she called her father in Puerto Rico and told him that I had a gambling habit, and everything is getting cut off in the house.

First he wired the money, and then moved to the United States with the promises of things getting better for us, even though we weren't going to be together,

In five years, damn near my whole family moved up here and they all became married to the life of drug dealing. I found a job at Greyhound as a driver, not wanting any parts of the criminal activities, and got sucked into it anyway. My husband got involved with dealers that had whole states on lock, and my basement became the stash spot. I can't even explain, but all I know is that damn Diamond's done robbed a armor truck and got away with the money and then when they found her later, she was dead.

They came to search my home for any stolen money and ended up finding two hundred and seven bricks of raw cocaine, along with three hundred thousand dollars. I'm so hurt to the point I might take my own life, because I also have to explain why I have the ID of a man that was tied up and murdered a year ago. I'm fucked all the way around the board, and now they got me sitting in this cold ass room on a twenty-four-hour hold, while they search for more evidence. I'm wondering if my husband Carlos, got this news, because this body is on their side of the fence, and if he doesn't man up to this shit, I will make the sky fall on his ass.

CHAPTER 11

The ride back to Philadelphia is a quiet ride. This is some backwards shit; first, I was feeling like I'm going to turn myself in or some shit, but now I'm kinda feeling like we should take the gamble. We need a house somewhere out east bubbafuck, but spending the money we have on a house can cripple our bankroll, so fuck it. I just hope for the best out this situation. "So Karen, this dude is a thorough dude, knowing he on the run with a reward and all that shit. He's super homie nigga, huh?"

"Okay, we're a team now, right?"
"Yeah, we a team."

"Okay, well, I know this nigga, Cargo, still wants to fuck me, so it kinda gives me leeway to his loyalty. So what I might do is lie to the nigga, telling him you're my cousin, just to get what I need done. I need him to think it's still a chance I will have sex with him, instead of him feeling funny around us, and we can save this nigga for a late night snack if our funds run low. After we sell this shit, I'm done and if we go broke, we just got to set it off or some shit."
"Well, we won't be setting nothing off, Karen, shit you tryna get us thrown under the jail somewhere?

That late night snack sounds good though, because we can make Cargo lead us to his connects and let that be that."

"It's a damn shame we got to think like this, but look what type of shit we in, Amin. I'm not a bad girl at all; it's just that when this game of survival got our backs against the wall, you just become unpredictable towards life, so what more can I say?"

"You ain't never lied, because I can't imagine me needing something to eat and can't afford it. Fuck begging; I'm taking a nigga whole life savings or either his life, because I feel like we headed for the chambers anyway. We either going to die in a shoot-out or lethal injection, you already know, Karen."

"Okay, Amin, we're almost here now. What are we doing, is we pulling up in this Benz, or are we parking and jump in a family cab?"

"It would make sense, but we going to need him waiting on us, because I'm not walking these streets with this high profile case we done caught. I know we on broke niggaz minds, as well as the whole town watching, and everybody else that's itching to see us, Karen, so be careful with impatient decision making."

"Fuck it; he just going to have to come pick us up from a truck stop and drop us back off. Shit, that's the best decision I can make right now."

"Okay, but let me find out you about to go fuck this nigga and become butt buddies, just so we can sell this coke."

"Nope, not at all, but I think you should've had a job making people laugh since you that funny, Amin. Who the fuck you think you talking to, besides the bitch who fell in love with you? I'm a prize to any man lucky enough to get in this pussy. See, just 'cause I fucked you on sight don't mean that's me. I just did that for guilt to ease down the pain this nigga put me through and luckily, you took me away from the memories I had with this chump. Amin, you made me happy within three hours and it tells me something good about you, because baby, I never got swept off my feet by a broke nigga. Don't get mad, because the ticket out of poverty is knowing the truth, loyalty will bless you all by itself. That's what got me, your first impression was making me feel like I had something I could call my own, so you didn't need a dime. You understand me, baby?"

"Well damn, okay. I just asked a question."

"Make me feel like I'm some whore again and I'm gon' see if you can fight as good as you can fuck, nigga."

"Go right ahead, because I ain't smacked me a bitch in two days. Sike, I'm joking; I don't hit women."

"Matter of fact, Amin, we gonna have this meeting in the car with this nigga, because I'm scared to get out and show my face. Seems like everybody knows me now."

Watching how main man comes out the crib I see already he's a draw box because niggas that's getting long money dress average not extra, this nigga really got a RUN DMC chain on like, nigga, is you about to bus' a rhyme? But my way of thinking has changed since we met this nigga, Cargo, because he's on the run from the feds and that alone brought us closer. He actually wants to run with us and we'll all be on the run together, drug dealing. However, I don't think Cargo knows what he getting himself into, fucking with two killers. He really has no advantage by turning us in, unless he coming to jail with us, and shit, where they do that at? "

I'm listening to Cargo and Karen trade opinions about these two kilos; this nigga is offering sixty thousand more than the shit is worth. Now, he's getting my attention, because who in their right mind will do some shit like that, and Karen is blind to these street games. But at the end of the day I guess he's paying for his presence to be in our company; I just hope Karen knows what she's doing.

"Well shit, Cargo, we had plans on setting up shop down south and come up off some country money."
Shit it's my turn. "Okay Cargo, I have a question, and that question be like, do you have a chick to go on this mission with you?"

"Hell yeah, my nigga, I got bitches that help me pull more bitches. Karen tell your boy about me,

I have a small circle when it comes to these niggas, because it's impossible for everybody to be on the same page, everybody don't have the same dreams…uh, my bad, what's your name again?"

"I'm her cousin, Amin; well shit Cargo bring the ugly ones, because one too many bad bitches is gonna still turn a cop's eye; they human too."

"Karen, your cousin is funny as shit, but the funniest part is that it makes sense, but still, I never heard no shit like that."

"Well, let us get situated and see how we can do this, because you been getting money for years, and it ain't no telling who they got looking for you. Worst case scenario, is you willing to kill for your freedom, nigga?" "I don't know, Karen, because when they catch me from this money laundering warrant, I'm coming home one day. I understand how y'all riding, but I can't say right now."

"Amin, what you think about how he sound?"

"Well, we need a lot of cash and we can roll the dice until we crap out, but that don't mean until we get locked up, because in this drug game you in, you gotta know when to fold 'em anyway. So what about fake ID's and a business, barber shops, and sneaker stores? It's not supposed to take this Glock to bust your head open for ideas homie."

"Okay, Amin, he got where you coming from. Cargo, I agree with Amin. We can ride with you for a smarter purpose now, because your heat can burn us down. Do you still feel the same way about this?"

"Karen, all I needed was a team like y'all. I'm good wit' it, but listen; take this eighty-thousand and get low. Ya boy, Cargo, about to get this ID thang lined up for tomorrow, so shit, it's on and popping, let's get it."

THREE MONTHS LATER

As time moves along, I'm kinda liking this dude, Cargo. He likes nice things and introduced us to a lot of connects and good people, he now knows that me and Karen are actually in a relationship, instead of cousins. Karen had to keep it real with him in order for him to understand. We all have our own cars now, and Karen and I stay together. I have a BMW 750i that stays parked, while we get around in Karen's hot pink Escalade. Cargo, I guess, just has to make himself hot no matter where he goes. How the fuck you young with no job, pushing a Rolls Royce in the hood? In a way, I was thinking he was trying to impress Karen. Deep down inside, I know he wants to fuck her, but you never know why people do dumbshit. But whatever; I'm just glad we're finally stable. My Aunt Rose took a deal for twenty-five years for kingpin status and needed to sell the house to somebody she could buy it back from, so for now, I can sleep. Cargo left us with two Asian chicks, Tia and Toka, to do all the dirty work. It was Karen's idea for us to become part of his plan to keep that bread coming in, and so far, things are working out, especially how he has girls walking around the house half naked, this nigga showing me something on the low.

"Umm…excuse me, Toka, can you put some fuckin' clothes on around my man? You ain't been swimming yet, but you wanna keep gliding past in a two-piece, tryna show my man that lil flat ass you working with."

"I'm sorry, K, if I intimidate you, but I don't want your man. I just like to get comfortable at night."

"Yeah whatever, and Amin, let me catch you tip-toeing, nigga. Matter of fact, Toka, you and your funny-looking ass sister about to move in the basement somewhere."

"Karen, if you run them away, we gon' have to do this shit by ourselves; that's something we don't want to do, so calm the fuck down."

"Yeah, I hear you, but let it be the other way around; you'd have twins, nigga."

I was wondering if Karen's jealousy would show one day, due to the fact that these bitches is on her level of beauty. Let alone the fact that they walk around half naked around me. Truth be told, they mainly get comfortable when Karen is upstairs counting money, but now I guess my baby's wondering what state of mind I'm in.

"Amin, can you put some soul food together, like some greens, mashed potatoes, turkey wings and yams for your woman? Shit, I know you know a lil something, homeslice."

"Homeslice? Damn, I ain't heard that one in years, but alright, go pull them wings out. Karen, where is Cargo? Does he know Baltimore like that?"

"No he just like to joy ride with bitches and show off, and get high. If he had brains, he could've been out the game, but you know how some niggas just like to floss. He's a hotel nigga, good trickin' ass nigga, and that's why I never fucked with him, just because he offered me money. But he do him, so you know."

"Oh well, okay whatever, Karen. I'm gonna need some vinegar with these greens and some more seasonings to bring this thing together, you heard me, young buck?"

"Well, you know where shit at out here, so where we off to, Amin?"

"They got a market called Shoppers out here that's got what we need and some more shit. Let's take the BMW out today for a joy ride."

"Amin, I know you love your car, but it's an eye catcher, baby. See, a female in a pink Escalade wouldn't be so bad, because okay, it's less heat, but a black nigga in a BMW 740i? That's a drug dealer's special, because you don't fit the description of a nerd anymore. You know you lean when you're driving. Yeah, again, it's an eye catcher."

"Whatever, I'll just find me a Tahoe or something that's gonna give me a work look then.

When I'm in your pink truck, it just seems to everybody on the outside looking in, like you're wearing the pants. Ohhh, but if they could only hear what comes out your mouth when I'm in that pussy."

"I don't know what you send through my body when you start talking dirty, but it turns me on. Now I'm in a different state of mind, so now what's getting ready to happen is this. I'm about to get dropped off, and I'm headed to Victoria's Secret. I'm getting sexy for the situation."

"Yeah, just don't let that GPS bullshit you, then wanna call me for directions, because right there, you might be shit out of luck. I know how to get to selective places out here, but go for what you know, Karen."

Sometimes just being observant can be a joy, because today is a nice day. White folks is jogging and walking their dogs, black folks got the chess boards out talking shit, while the kids is hop-scotching and playing double dutch. Mother Nature is feeling good, so we feeling good, she's giving us good sunshine and it's 70-degrees with a breeze you wish you had all year long.

I see this good day jumped in Karen, because now she wanna get dressed for the situation. On that note, I already know she wanna rub all on a nigga, kiss on me and make them sexy ass moans in my ear, causing that clear shit to come out a nigga, and I heard it's the precum that gets them pregnant.

The way I'm visualizing it, if she busts out in one of them outfits, lip gloss shining, and smelling like a fresh shower, then yeah, bitch, you're definitely gonna be my slut today Shit, we gon' kiss and express our emotions physically with detailed affection, and then I'm grab a handful of that good ass hair she got, and take the hardest dick in the world and play in her mouth with it and shit. If she add the sound effects, then round two is going in the pussy, because I know them dick suck noises going to make a nigga unload everything in me. I'm not talking about regular noises; it's them freak ass noises that sound like it tastes so damn good to her, sheesh.

SHOPPER SUPERMARKET

Karen's been in her own lil world ever since I stopped talking, so ain't no telling what she's planning for later. I know one thing, I'm ready to get up out this market; I can't stand shopping with women, they take all day. Like right now, the cart is full to the top and she's still looking at shit.

"Aye Karen, you put one more thing in that cart and we gon' fight, because damn, we been in here for a hour already, Shit. What we came for was some seasoning, but you got enough in that cart to last us six months. Now come on bring that ass to the cash register."

"I know, Amin, I'm sorry but you know how this is, you come for one thing and you see everything else you need. Don't get mad at me; you know we can't be running back and forth, so I'm just going hard right now. Calm down before I get loud in this muthafucka."

"Bitch, bust a move."

"I'm gon' bust a move on that ass, alright."

It seems as if my baby has her mind made up, all singing and shit, and just cause she's happy, I'm satisfied.

"Okay, we're finally out the market, you satisfied? Or do I need to think of something else I need? Because I just feel like fucking with you now, make you mad, and then throw your dick in my mouth just to see how fast you change your attitude, you freak ass, nigga."

"Whatever, I'm hungry for real now, Karen. Shit done changed; I need you over that stove in something sexy."

"No Amin, you said you were gonna play chef today, stop playing."

"Okay… okay… okay… I was only playing."

Back in the house getting the cabinets filled, I keep hearing something or somebody moving around upstairs. I'm headed for my Glock to go do my paranormal activity investigation, with my heart beating faster than a muthafucka and since it's wall-to-wall carpeting, my creep game is on pro.

When I get all the way up there, come to find out, either Tia or Toka is in their room getting dressed or something. I thought, fuck it while I'm up here, I might as well take a shower, throw my Versace pajamas on, and get prepared for a damn good time. We got Moët and all kinds of liquor my aunt left in here, so it's on. All set and ready for the water sports, I'm armed with Coast soap, fresh Hanes and a wife beater, with a good song to sing while I'm in there.

"Oh no, you ain't getting ready to get in my bath water, Amin."

"Damn Tia, you scared the shit outta me, girl. I didn't see your car outside, so I thought you wasn't home but fo' sho' I'm up in this shower."

"Well, we just gonna be in there together then, because I gotta go."

When I get in the bathroom, I see she did run her water, but since the shower is separate, it still can happen. I just hope Karen doesn't walk in on this part. Damn, I just noticed this shower don't have a curtain, but oh well, fuck it; she just gotta wait.

I'm trying to be as quick as possible on my John Wayne shit, I brush the water off my face to see Tia standing in front of me naked. "Damn Tia, you could've waited." "Amin, tell me something; why your girlfriend don't like us?"

"Shit y'all look good and she probably feels intimidated by your beauty, but can you not ask me some shit you already know?"

"Well, tell me why you didn't try to cover yourself up when you noticed me standing here?"

Before I could answer, Tia came in the shower, got on her knees and grabbed my dick. Then she told me dreams do come true and then started with just sucking the head looking for a reaction of pleasure.

I'm fucked up in the head by her actions, so I gotta dumb look on my face, because this lil bitch is bad, with her suntan complexion, the sexy bedroom eyes, and the lips she got, damn, they fit a mean dick suck. I grabbed Tia by the hand and took her to her room, laid her down then lifted them lil legs up and before I can get halfway in, she's screaming and got her fucking nails in my neck. Man, since this gotta be a quickie, I'm going deep.

"Aaahhh...aaahhh...ooohhh! Baby, fuck me, fuck me, fuck me, fuck me!"

This pussy is so tight. I can tell she ain't doing too much fuckin', but shit, I can't cum fast though because she sounds so sexy. Now that this dick in all her, I wanna hear what else she gon' scream out. Finally, I'm all the way in and this pussy is dynamite and wet and the louder she screams, the more paranoid I get, because I can't hear if anybody's coming up the stairs. Wow, I so can't get caught like this, Karen will kill me. I wanna see how far she gon' let me go, so I ask, "Let me put it in your ass, Tia?"

"Whatever you want me to do, I will do, baby. I wish you were mine," Tia moans, and I know I got her just where I want her.

Now I'm knee deep in this ass and she sound like she's possessed. I'm ramming this dick so far in her ass, trying to bust a nut off her screams.

I'm pumping harder and faster, and then boom, I hit the jackpot finally. "Aaawwwee shit!" I groan, while she's moaning.

"Ooohh, damn, you fuck me so good, baby!"

"Sheesh…Damn girl, that was nice, but now you got to get your shit and get the fuck out, because you're not gonna be looking at me all funny when my baby around. I know you gonna be looking with your 'want to fuck again' looks; she catches on too fast for that sneaky shit."

"Well, who told you to fuck me, you freak ass nigga? That's just why I couldn't care less about a relationship now. You niggas ain't shit and you just proved it."

"Aye Tia, you need a fuckin' bag in your hand, or your whole body going in one."

"Amin, is you serious?"

"Don't call me by my name like you know me either. See, that's exactly what the fuck I'm talking 'bout. Bitch, you rich, so get the fuck out, Tia."

"I don't get this shit. Nigga, if you gon' be that fucking paranoid, why don't you just stay loyal?"

"The most important part about this story, Tia, is you packing your shit and saying goodbye with a smile on your face.

Other than that, you're making me nervous, woman."

"I don't believe this shit; this got to be the funniest episode ever. Damn okay, I'm gonna leave, but I'll be back, nigga, just taking a lil vacation."

"Tia, just leave."

Damn, now my shower has to be a fast one and shit. I got to pop a vitamin to help me out with Karen, because me and this bitch in the house at the same time with a fifty percent dick, equals me cheating. Lord knows, the last thing I wanna do is see her with that "I ain't dumb" look on her face, mixed with her looking like she wants to cry. Sometimes I feel like a lover boy, because when I'm with you, it's all about you. At the same time, this only takes me back to how I already feel, like if a nigga always around my girl, it's a chance they can become more than just friends, because temptation gets into you without your own permission. Yeah, I could've controlled it, but sometimes shit just takes you by surprise. With this Dark and Lovely shampoo running down my face, I'm feeling the withdrawal of betrayal setting in on me, and I just hope I can keep myself from looking stupid when I first catch eye contact.

That dumb look raise flags of curiosity. Fresh out the shower and feeling like a million bucks, I'm ready to slide up in my Versace pajama pants, with a fresh, bright white tank top to make it all right. Shit, there's a bottle of gin in my aunt's cabinet that's calling my name, so shit, I'm 'bout to get nice. I won't be looking dumb for the rest of the night, I'm thinking, but as I'm coming downstairs to finish out my plan, I see four female legs. The further I get down the stairs, I find out I'm easing into a conversation on why Tia is leaving, and Karen is the host.

"Amin, did Tia tell you anything about a vacation?"

"Naw, why she going on vacation?"

"She said she told you about it."

"Karen, she probably did, but my mind is somewhere else right now."

"Well, did you leave it in this bitch's pussy, Amin? Because why all of a sudden, she thought I was a ghost when she saw me. And why were you in the shower so long?"

"Well damn, am I allowed to take a good shit before I get in the shower, or did I need to call you and let you know to stop your timer, until that last ball fall out my ass? Karen, just cut it out."

"Ain't no 'cut it out', there's a reason why this bitch looked all nervous when she saw me, because any other time, it's 'hey girl, you okay', and all that homie-homie shit. Don't fucking play with me, but okay Amin, I hope you ain't feeling pimpish, muthafucka."

"Girl, get a grip! So Tia, that's what it is, a vacation?"

"Not so much of a vacation, but I met somebody that I can't get off my mind, Amin. The late night conversations is kinda making me curious of how it would be spending a week or two with him, you feel me?"

"Well, Tia, when I asked you, why you couldn't just say that?" Karen asked.

"Because, Karen…please don't get offended, but I like you and just in case you liked me too, I didn't want to mess it up, by telling you how I'm about to go fuck somebody else."

I'm trying to find my jaw, because that muthafucka just dropped and probably rolled up under something. I wasn't expecting her to just bust out the closet and say that, but that's nice to know. Shit, now I want to talk her into saying fuck the vacation, but that might not sit right with Karen.

"Oh my God, so you saying you have it your way with me in your head at night, Tia?"

"I got to go, Karen, I'll see y'all when I come back." I'm already in the kitchen with a glass of gin, I found my jaw, but it still hangs a little. What the fuck did she say again?

I'm feeling more comfortable since Karen got some other shit on her mind, but damn, one thing I see you can't take from a man, is the attraction he has for his woman. Just being around her again, I can feel that connection locking back in, along with the plans we had laid out for this innocent night Mother Nature blessed us with. The streets are calm, the sky is settled with a full moon and when I look outside, I see the old folks sitting out on their front porches, reminiscing about shit that happened in the sixties. Now, by the time this gin gets all the way through my system, midnight should be arriving in just enough time for 95.9 to start bumping them old school classics to get us in that 'staring at each other' mood. After that, then shit, you already know.

"Amin, I got lobster tails, shrimps, crabmeat, salad and more. I was hoping you were upstairs chillin', because I wanted to surprise you with decorations, but shit, it won't take me long."

"It's all good, baby, do ya thang. I ain't going nowhere."

"But did you hear Tia? She basically came at me and you didn't say not a mothafuckin' thing, nigga. I just hope that didn't put no kind of imagination in your head on some 'me you and her' shit, because it ain't happening, captain."

"Get on your knees and put this dick in your mouth, and show me how tonight can be."

"Nigga, you crazy. That shit you drinking sound good, but I'm busy and tonight don't last forever. You can come snack on this pussy though, and show me what new tricks you learned, because damn, boy, for a beginner, you sure know how to keep me lookin' at your freak ass."

Before I could respond, I noticed Cargo coming in out the corner of my eye, not looking so happy since the last time we were together.

"Hey...hey, what's good y'all?"

"What's good, Cargo, we on some MIA shit now?"

"Karen, y'all probably be on y'all own from here. They done fucked around and ran up in my mom crib and found everything. She didn't know it was in there and if I don't turn myself in within twenty-four hours, they gonna charge her with all that shit. The feds got my number and keep calling me, and I'm stressed to the max."

"Well, before you turn yourself in, let's go out and have a nice time!"

"Amin, I won't be able to enjoy myself, but fuck it, when y'all ready?"

"Shit, now!"

I wonder if Karen got the same thing in mind as I do, because she said, "Now", as fast as I did. It's sad to say, but Cargo won't be going to jail; he's going to his grave.

"Amin, just put on what you just took off. I'm already dressed." We hop in the truck and I'm thinking as fast as I can. First, we gotta "rob" this nigga and leave a couple dollars in his pocket, so it won't look like a homicide robbery, and then just off this nigga. I don't know who I've become, but I know we can't afford for this dude to get in there with a special offer like throwing us under the bus for a lesser sentence. I'm going up on this bottle of gin like it's a cold Pepsi, because deep down, I hate to keep on this way, but what I'm wondering is why the fuck he come tell us this shit, like we ain't a prize catch.

"Aye, look y'all, fuck it. The only move I have left is to leave y'all everything and y'all just keep getting it and feed my lawyers what they need. I'm not new to this jail shit, but ain't no telling the outcome of this, but since money talk, we gon' see what it's gon' do, feel me? So while we at this bar, club, or whatever I'm gon' have somebody bring me everything I have in my house, money and all. Depending on when they get out here, that's when we leave, deal?"

"That sounds good to me; how about you, Karen?"

"It sound good, but Cargo, can we trust you not to get scared and rat us out, nigga.?"

Why would I give you my money first? I'm 'bout to bring you sixty thousand dollars to keep it moving. In this game, who could you really trust besides the people in the same situation as you and shit? If I get a bail, my mom can bail me out; just get the bread to her before something else comes up and stops me from getting out. Don't go there, because I need y'all."

Cargo just talked his life back in his hands, but still I gotta wait 'til the smoke clears about this nigga.

"Well shit, fuck the club, just make them moves and have your ammunition on deck, Cargo."

"You right, Amin, I'm on that."

CHAPTER 12

Now that we got the money phone, this muthafucka is ringing off the hook and we have damn near sixteen kilos for the customers. This shit is scary as hell, being a real drug dealer, because I don't have a clue on who these muthafuckas is Cargo hooked us up with. I feel like we the only ones selling this shit.

"Karen, we got to make these people travel for this shit, because I don't feel safe knowing this nigga in there talking to them people. Shit, I don't know the nigga and he can say 'fuck us' easy, so we outta here."

"Amin, I guess great minds think alike, because I be damn if I wasn't thinking the same way. Yeah, we can bail him out; we just gonna kill him when he comes home and keep all this shit, because that nigga ain't got no love for me. He just wanted to see his dick in my mouth, he moved Toka in with him to be his sex slave with a for sale sign on her at the same damn time, he's about a dirty freak."

We got Tia to set up our stay at the Marriott Hotel when she got back off her bullshit vacation, just in case them folks got plans on catching us with our drawers down. I did put her on to really take a vacation, 'til we become eye-to-eye with the situation, but if Cargo man's up to all he said, then I don't think we should kill him. I do know one thing for sure though, this bitch, Karen, is evil for real.

THREE WEEKS LATER

This hotel room is so luxurious, it's to the point I wish this was our home. We've been laying low for a nice minute now, just by keeping it moving casually. I can feel the curiosity coming from employees that work here, and for some odd reason, the butterflies is back in my fucking stomach. I wonder if it's just me knowing we have over a million dollars in this room with five kilos left, or is it this one white customer we have that makes me wonder about him, every time he cop up, his body language is not sensitive towards what can happen, while he's buying a half brick at a time. He's just too smooth with his t-shirt tucked in, looking like a fucking cop and now I'm wondering how long Cargo's been hustling off this one phone, because we just might have a hot ass phone.

The money phone begins to ring, pulling me out of my thinking zone, and the look on Karen's face is a worried one as she talks to a customer. I can't wait for her to tell me the mission. "Oh okay, we'll be there shortly. Just be by the side of the gallery, next to the hotdog stand off Market Street." She ends the call.

"What's the deal, baby?"

"Amin, it's the white guy, Charley. He just made me fucking nervous, because he just bought a half brick just three days ago, but now he just said he needs two kilos and if I had more, to bring it. What kind of shit was that, 'if I had more just bring it'? When it comes to white drug dealers, okay, the smart ones ain't too flashy, but it's just something about this Charley nigga, Amin, that just don't sit right with me."

My personal cell phone rings, and the poison begins to flow through my ears. It's Mom, telling me all the cops in the world is on the lookout for me, because my father told the police I'm moving from state to state, and that it would only help me out if I turned myself in.

"Mom, they gotta work for they money; I'm not turning myself into them. I didn't do anything, and Mom, just remember that I love you dearly, just in case things don't turn out right."

"Where are you now, Amin?"

"I'm in Brooklyn, New York."

"Well, why they say they know you're here in Philadelphia, and it would be easier for you to turn yourself in, instead of them catching you?"

Those words just made me dizzy; I feeling closed in, and after I hang up on my mom, I turned my phone off. I'm sweating now, because the fucking heat is really on now.

"Amin, come on, let's go get this money and damn, what's wrong with your face?"

"Nothing; I'll tell you after this mission."

The closer we get to the double doors to get out, all types of things are going on in my body. I gotta shit, I just farted, I'm feeling like I'm ready to throw up, and I'm really trying to hold this shit down. "Amin did you tell Charley where we was at?"

"No why?"

"Because that's Charley double-parked across the street, looking over here at us!"

"Let's go back and hurry up! Come on, we going up the fire escape."

I take a glance back and see nothing but ATF agents, along with regular uniformed police, screaming and shoving people out their way as they're coming up behind us. I found the fire escape, but when I pulled it; it set the alarms off.

"Damn what the fuck! Ummm…like hellooo…get rid of that bag, Karen!"

"Oh shit, Amin, they coming up behind us!"

"Just keep coming, baby!"

"It's nowhere else to run, Amin, that's the roof exit."

"Well, we on the roof, but you still carrying that jail bag though."

Now on the roof with only a twenty-second head start on the law, time is running out. This hot ass Cargo got us caught up in his bullshit. I guess I should've thought on it a lil while longer, because the feds want convictions only, so their homework is getting solid evidence before they even lock you up. All Cargo kept seeing was the money, but oh well. The Fed screams, "Freeze! Get on the fucking ground! Don't make me shoot y'all muthafuckas! I haven't shot me a nigger in years, so don't make me now!" Piss is beginning to run down Karen's leg like a water hose is tucked in her waist, and I'm mad because this muthafucka just said he ain't shot a nigger in years.

"You ready, Karen?"

"R-r-ready for what, baby?" Karen looks me and notices the tears in my eyes rolling down my face.

"Give me your hand; we getting ready to jump."

"I'm gonna ask you one more time to get on the fucking ground!" Another fed yells.

Looking at how far we about to jump is making me want to change my mind and let them lock me up. The people look so small, they look like walking toys. Nothing matters right now, so fuck the police and their bullets; we're dead one way or the other.

As I continue to look down, out of nowhere, Karen screams from the top of her lungs and before I could look to see what's wrong, it's too late; we're over the edge dream. I can hear people screaming,

"Oh my God", loud and clear, along with Karen's screams as we're falling, still holding hands. We're falling like we're on a ride at Great Adventures somewhere, love stands alone because we are falling to our deaths, but I still want to make sure she doesn't get hurt. Lord, I ask you to forgive me for my sins, forgive me for not knowing what was more important, forgive us for deciding to die, before we got punished for something we didn't do, in the name of Jesus, Amen...

Made in the USA
Middletown, DE
11 January 2023

21330879R00070